MARGE PIERCY

PM PRESS OUTSPOKEN AUTHORS SERIES

PM PRESS OUTSPOKEN AUTHORS SERIES

My Life, My Body

plus...

My Life, My Body

plus

much more

and

"Living Off the Grid"

Outspoken Interview

Marge Piercy

PM PRESS | 2015

"A Dissatisfaction without a Name." *Click: Becoming Feminists*, edited by Lynn Crosbie. Toronto: Macfarlane, Walter & Ross Publishers, 1997.

"The More We See the Less We Know." *Los Angeles Times*, March 24, 2004.

"What they call acts of god." *Monthly Review* 65, no. 1, May 2013.

"Statement on Censorship for the *Pennsylvania Review*." *Pennsylvania Review*.

"Fame, Fortune and Other Tawdry Illusions." *Boston Review* 6, no. 1, February 1982.

"Housewives without Houses." Syndicated by the *New York Times*, August 1994.

"The hows; there is no why" was published online in the Red Beard Anthology, 2014.

"Touched by Ginsberg at a (Relatively) Tender Age." *Paterson Literary Review* 35, January 2006.

"Tabula Rasa with Boobs." *All the Available Light: A Marilyn Monroe Reader*, edited by Yona McDonough. New York: Touchstone Books, 2002.

"Why Speculate on the Future?" *Envisioning the Future: Science Fiction and the Next Millennium*, edited by Marleen S. Barr. Middletown, CT: Wesleyan University Press, 2003.

"Behind the war on women." *Narrative Northeast*, January 2014.

"Never Catch a Break." *Michigan Quarterly Review* 27, no. 1, Winter 1988; and in *Subversions: Anarchist Short Stories*, vol. 2, foreword by Marge Piercy. Montreal: Anarchist Writers Bloc, 2012.

"The Port Huron Conference Statement" was delivered at a conference in Ann Arbor in 2012 called A New Insurgency: The Port Huron Statement in Its Time and Ours, 50th Anniversary.

"Who has little, let them have less." *Monthly Review* 65, no. 8, January 2014.

Original to this volume: "Headline: Lawmaker destroys shopping carts," "Gentrification and Its Discontents," "Nice words for ugly acts," and "My Life, My Body." All Copyright Marge Piercy, 2015

My Life, My Body, Marge Piercy © 2015
This edition © 2015 PM Press
Series editor: Terry Bisson

ISBN: 9781629631059
Library of Congress Control Number: 2015930892

Outsides: John Yates/Stealworks.com • Insides: Jonathan Rowland

PM Press • P.O. Box 23912 • Oakland, CA 94623

10 9 8 7 6 5 4 3 2 1

Printed in the USA by the Employee Owners of Thomson-Shore in Dexter, Michigan
www.thomsonshore.com

CONTENTS

A DISSATISFACTION
WITHOUT A NAME

WHEN DID I FIRST become a feminist? I suspect it was around puberty, when I began to think hard about what I saw in my family and around me.

My mother had been sent to work as a chambermaid when she was still in the tenth grade, because her family was large and poor and needed the income she could bring in. She had an active mind, a strong sense of politics and an immense curiosity. She read a great deal, haphazardly. She had no framework of knowledge of history or economics or science in which to fit what she read or what she experienced, so that intelligent observations jostled superstitions and folk beliefs. She was a mental magpie, gathering up and carrying off to mull over anything that attracted her attention, anything that glittered out of the ordinary boredom of being a housewife. There was, truly, something birdlike about her, a tiny woman (only four feet ten) with glossy black hair who would cock her head to the side and stare with bright dark eyes.

She had grown up in a radical Jewish family where politics was discussed and debated. She had a sense of class conflict and social reality that was the most consistent and logical part of her mind. My father could easily be seduced by racism, sexism, Republican promises of lowering taxes. Like many working class men of his time, he started out on the left and moved steadily toward the right. My mother never wavered in her analysis of who was on her side and who was not. She trusted few politicians, but she appreciated those she thought fought for the rights of ordinary people.

My father very much enjoyed sexist jokes and told them till the end of his life, ignoring my attitudes if I was present. They were a way of knocking on the wooden reality of how things were with men and women and showing how sound it was. My mother did not tell such jokes and seldom laughed at them. However, she had attitudes of her own. She admired women who fought for other women, but she also had contempt for women. She complained of women's weakness, at the same time that she herself had few strengths to fall back on. She viewed sex as a powerful force that carried off women into servitude. A woman's sexuality was a tremendous force that exacted a lifelong price from her.

When I was little, I thought of my mother as very strong—for certainly she had power over me. My father would punish me severely, with fists and feet and a wooden yardstick. But my mother was usually the one who set the rules, since my father did not take much interest, except sometimes to decide I must do something I didn't want to do, because he had contempt for cowards: climb a ladder to the roof, cross a narrow high footbridge. These demands had little to do with me, but were part of a war between them. She had many fears (he was driving too fast, too dangerously) that in some way pleased him. Her fear proved he was strong and able, in comparison to my mother (whom he never taught to drive). But I was the battleground in which he demonstrated how women were afraid by demanding I do things I feared.

So I learned to do them. I learned to overcome my fear and do foolhardy things never without thinking but without giving an outward sign of my fear. I did it partly in a futile effort to gain his respect, which could never be granted. That respect was never attainable because of my sex and because my mother and I were Jewish, and he was not. He was not anything in particular. He thought of himself as English, Anglo-Saxon, but he was only one quarter English; he was half Welsh and one quarter Scottish. He was far more a Celt than an Anglo-Saxon. He was a moody man who feared and denied emotions; they were what he regarded as sins. He liked to drink; he liked to eat what he regarded as proper masculine food (meat and potatoes mostly); he liked to play poker and other card games. But he intensely disliked being aware that he felt anything except anger. His anger was swift and thunderous. He never hit my mother but he frightened her. Again, I was the surrogate. He could and did hit me. Also my older brother.

My mother had a temper of her own. She got angry as quickly as he did. She had a far more vivid vocabulary of curses, some in Yiddish (used only with me), most in English. "Shit and molasses!" she would yell. "Piss blood and drink it!" Her temper was released on me, of course, and on objects. I remember her at the kitchen table pulling the cloth laden with supper—dishes and food and flowers—and throwing it against the wall. She broke dishes with abandon. Never the good dishes. No, she broke the mismatched dishes she got as giveaways at the movies or bought at garage and yard sales.

She was not a middle-class lady. She cursed, she thought of herself as fastidious but wasn't, she lost her temper, she liked bright colors and gaudy objects. She was overtly sexual. She was immensely curious and loved plants and animals. She was always hungry for conversation, for communication, for something of interest. My early and middle childhood centered around her. My father was dangerous but peripheral. When I was young, I could not understand why she never seemed to get what she wanted.

I remember a particular birthday of hers, which came in November, the year I turned thirteen. My mother always fussed about presents. She would shop carefully for my father, sometimes buying his gift several months in advance. She liked to give presents and she desperately enjoyed being given them. I always gave her as nice presents as I could afford. That went on until she died at eighty-seven (we think). I still have many of them.

For her birthday, my father gave her a new garbage can for the kitchen and a broom. She wept for hours. There was not only boredom in the gift but insult. I brooded over this, wherein lay the insult. I said to her, why don't you buy yourself what you want? Why does he have to give it to you? Why don't you go out and buy yourself a good red dress, a new coat, a leather purse? She looked at me as if I was crazy and said, "He'd never put up with me spending that kind of money on myself."

"What business is it of his what you spend money on?"

Again she glared at me, an idiot child. "It isn't my money."

I began then to understand why my mother had to defer to my father, why my mother could yell and sulk and wheedle and brood but could never win. She worked all the time, obviously, but the only money she had was what he gave her for the house. They quarreled constantly about how much she spent on groceries. Everything was controlled by him. He bought himself a new car every two or three years, but there was no money for me to go to the dentist. My teeth rotted in my mouth and broke off. It wasn't until I was putting myself through college that I spent much of my first semester sitting in the dental school having my teeth fixed by student dentists. He owned every power tool he saw advertised. I went off to college without a winter coat. My mother developed cataracts but never saw an eye doctor. At eighty-seven, she was still cleaning the house without help.

When I was fifteen, they moved to a bigger house in Detroit, where she began to rent out rooms. Now she had money of her own, finally, which she could use as she pleased. But it was too late. She said to me, "I can't leave him now. The house is in his name. I'd starve."

When my mother was eighty-six, she demanded that we drive down to Florida because she had a present to give me too big for us to carry back on the plane. She did give me a box of silver-plate that would easily have fit in a suitcase, but what she really wanted to give me waited until my father went out. Then out of hiding places all over their tiny house she pulled out single dollar bills, one after the other. For an hour she piled up dollar bills, until she had given us $1,200, stuffed in cracks in the floor, hidden in closets, thrust into coat pockets, under dresser scarves, in the bottom of dry vases. This was her immense bequest. She had saved this gift out of grocery money, squirreling it away, because she knew she was going to die soon (she had suffered a ministroke she had told no one about and soon would have another that would kill her) and she wanted to give me an inheritance. It had taken her immense effort to save and secrete these bills.

It became clear to me sometime between the ages of thirteen and fifteen that economics was the bedrock on which any independence had to be built. If I couldn't make a living, I would be as wretched as my mother. If I depended on a man to support me, I would be enslaved. It was that simple to me.

In contrast to my mother was my Aunt Ruth, who was midway between us in age. She worked. She had only a high school diploma, which kept her from advancing in the Navy when she worked for them, kept her from advancing up any corporate ladder. But she was bright, ambitious and she made a living. She took up bowling and won trophies. She was one of the only women jocks I knew. When she married and moved into a middle class suburb, she took up golf instead and soon she was filling the house with golf trophies. She was a far more observant Jew than my mother, but she was also more worldly. She dressed like a working woman and wore slacks—then a novelty. She had no children and she spent her money as she pleased, even after she married.

Her husband began to beat and abuse her. She had my grandmother living with her half a year and half with us. That complicated Ruth's choices. My mother said, Poor Ruth! What can she do? But Ruth cut through it all and ran off with another man who was much kinder to her and with whom she lived the rest of her life. She eloped, taking my grandmother with her. It was clear to me that if you earned your own money and you had the guts to do what you wanted, you would never be stuck—as my mother was.

I went through childhood and adolescence brooding a great deal about the war between women and men, about the inequalities I saw and did not want in my own life. I had no word for my concerns, no political framework in which to think about what I observed. For the next ten years, whenever I was involved with a man, I would eventually feel an enormous weight of despair. Both men and women told me that was how things were, unequal, and that I should accept the female situation with graceful acquiescence because it had always been so and would always be so: this was the message of high and low culture, from the novels and poetry we read to the messages of advertisements and men's and women's glossy and pulp magazines, the movies we went to, the songs played over the radio. Everything said, men are strong and women are weak, and women like it that way. Men rule and women are ruled, and women like it that way. Men earn money and women stay home and have babies and raise babies (and then what?) and spend money. Men think; women feel. Men plan; women flirt. Men do; women are done. Anything else was unnatural, and what could be worse than an unnatural woman?

By my last two years of college, I was a better writer than the men around me in writing classes and in the school journals. I had begun to win prizes. Prizes were, after all, won under sexless pseudonyms. Yet I never received the respect men my age did. I could not understand why I should not be taken seriously. I had no more affairs than many of the men in my circles, yet my few affairs were scandalous and I was a scarlet woman, a shameless hussy.

Similarly, I had no name for the invisibility that came over me when I married, left graduate school and began to work as a secretary to support my husband's graduate studies in physics. I was aware I had suddenly become invisible, inaudible, of no account. I spent a long time figuring that one out.

Then suddenly Simone de Beauvoir put it all in focus and gave me a name for my discontent. At twenty-two, I read *The Second Sex*. That amazing book provided the impetus to walk out of my marriage and rethink the choices I had made. I had a vocabulary in which I could define and retain insights that had come to me for years, but which the society had labeled crazy. I was not crazy, after all. Now I knew what I was: I was a feminist.

THE MORE WE SEE, THE LESS WE KNOW

IT MAY BE THAT television has addled our ability to choose a leader wisely. Between sound bites and the seduction of images we run a popularity contest every four years instead of an election.

Would Abraham Lincoln have a chance today? He was ugly. We like photogenic leaders. We want leaders who appear to be flawless in past and present, which limits the intelligence, curiosity and experience of our winning candidates. We prefer someone shallow to someone of wide and deep experience.

We have disqualified candidates for President and Vice President because they wept. Apparently an inability to feel something deeply is required for high office. Eagleton was bumped out of contention for Vice President because he had been smart enough to seek help when he needed it. Apparently we prefer untreated problems in our candidates. We respond to candidates as we have become accustomed to responding to celebrities: would we like them, do we find them attractive, can we identify with the character they project on the small or large screen?

We often appear more interested in the sexual adventures or the lack of them in our heroes than in their political positions, which would have cost Thomas Jefferson the presidency as well as Grover Cleveland, Franklin Delano Roosevelt and Dwight D. Eisenhower. Martin Luther King Jr. could not have led the civil rights movement if his affairs had been held against him. Sexual peccadilloes do not cost lives or wreck the economy.

Great leaders have always been flawed. Would Moses make it in sound bites? He stammered. He also was a felon and a fugitive. F.D.R. was severely handicapped. Dukakis looked like Rocky the Squirrel in a tank. We seem to believe that looking good in a military pose is far more important than having a grasp of what war actually involves to the invading country and the invaded. A sense of history would have helped immensely before we took on Iraq, but we are trained to mistrust men of ideas and obvious education. Our leaders should not appear to be smarter than we are.

The worst thing that a politician can be called is elitist—and what do we mean by that? In Iowa, Howard Dean was labeled that—a sushi eating, PBS watching, Volvo driving man—not macho enough, clearly, to win the vote of working men. But who determines the massive layoffs and the movement of corporations abroad that gut the economies of so many cities and drive families from comfort into chaos? Those are the members of the real elite, and they aren't defined by eating sushi or watching PBS. There is a class of people who send their sons to the "best" private schools and the Ivy League universities, who join the interlocking boards of corporations and become their CEOs. These are the people who move the jobs to India and to China and to Guam. They are the people who support the notion that intellectuals are dangerous and intelligence is elitist. Their political propaganda claims that people who own oil companies and drive up the prices you pay at the pump are just regular guys who love NASCAR and football and eat barbeque and Big Macs. These power brokers are just luckier more and photogenic versions of you.

Often the Bible gets quoted in political contexts. But do the people who quote it actually read it? Those Bible stories resonate for us because they are often about leaders and people with important destinies—but these men and women are not cartoon heroes. Saul would be in danger of commitment to a mental institution. David not only had an affair but got rid of the husband. Jacob deceived his father on his death bed. But they also overcame their flaws and in the long run, they carried forward a vision. It is that vision that makes them memorable and for that moral vision we still tell their stories.

Surely we could learn to vote in favor of those who will fight for our good, rather than the welfare of those who contribute heavily and profit from many governmental decisions. I wish we could learn to vote for our interests and not for the politician we think we would like best as our daddy or our pal.

Headline: Lawmaker destroys shopping carts

The homeless make him angry.
They're in the way. He doesn't
find them scenic. How dare they
survive on the street, in parks,
in alleys, doorways and beaches.

Making life even more difficult
for those at the end of choices
is his answer to their problems.
Euthanasia would likely please
him. Has he never lost a job?

Run out of money? Been robbed
or beaten? Never been hungrier
than a good steak fixed? He can't
understand how people scrape,
pick trash to survive, pushing

all that remains of their past
in a shopping cart. Their lives

aren't hard enough, he thinks,
planning how to vanish them
taking the little they have left.

GENTRIFICATION AND ITS DISCONTENTS

I LIVED IN THE tenth arrondissement of Paris, in the Gare de l'Est–Gare du Nord district bounded at the end of our block by the Saint-Martin Canal. Mostly commercial boats passed in both directions. It was a working-class neighborhood with small shops or small industries on the ground floor of most buildings. There were many poor Jews, poor native-born French, some born in Paris and some from Provence and the Auvergne, Hungarians and Poles. The shops were like the bodegas I was familiar with years later in Manhattan. They served the necessities of the neighborhood and a few luxuries—candy, tobacco. The wine store offered huge kegs of plonk. We brought our own bottles to be filled. The bistros were small and smoky but put out decent grub.

Years later when I was back in Paris, the neighborhood was inhabited by Algerians mostly, some Moroccans. The shops were just as shabby. One storefront was a mosque. The canal was the same, the hallways smelled a bit different but of equally real food.

The last time I visited my old stomping grounds, the storefronts were travel agencies, boutiques selling high-heeled shoes I would never wear or fashionable dresses for size 0 to 2, dry cleaners that also specialized in fine leather and furs, a wine store without kegs, several small elegant restaurants and some take-out places for professionals rushing home from work. The canal was much cleaner. The buildings lining it had been rehabbed. The Arab-speaking inhabitants had been shoved out to the banlieues. Where had the inhabitants of my old block gone? Into the ground, some. Who knows where the others live now . . .

In Chicago I lived on 55th Street over a place that distributed newspapers to vendors and deliverymen. We had six rooms cold in winter and hot in summer, but my roommate and I and our transitory companions could spread out without getting into one another's privacy—a good place for me to write. The rent was affordable so that I only had to work part-time and had the space and time to find myself as a poet. Across the street the Compass bar stood, where Shelley Berman, Elaine May and Mike Nichols, and many others had their start. It was the local bohemian hang-out and when the University of Chicago brought in urban renew-al, it was one of the first sites to be razed. Our building survived a year and a half longer. Everything that replaced it was new and shiny—by now not so immaculate but hardly bohemian.

In San Francisco, I lived on North Point Street in a two-room apartment over the garage with a corner sort-of kitchen. When the wind blew from the west, we smelled chocolate from the Ghirardelli factory. When the wind blew from the north, we smelled tomatoes form the cannery behind us. When the wind blew from the south, we smelled fish. Fisherman's Wharf, a very short walk away, was already something of a tourist trap but still had working fishing boats coming in and plenty of seafood for sale. A freight line ran up the middle of North Point and then veered off at our corner to service the cannery and fish-packing plant.

Our neighborhood was inhabited by straight and gay, hair-dressers, jazz musicians, artists, writers, potters, bartenders, conmen, some prostitutes, and people who had small shops nearby. The rent was cheap. In the supermarket two blocks down I could buy Chinese, Japanese, Italian groceries.

We were a casual and polyglot lot, mixed racially. In the vacant lot next door, wild fennel grew that I picked and used cooking the bags of artichokes I bought. I made friends with a number of the people in the neighborhood where we all lived because it was cheap and safe and friendly and ultimately convenient. The washing machine and dryer were on the roof, where I had a great view of the Golden Gate Bridge, Alcatraz, all the Bay and the fog rolling in almost every afternoon.

Nobody I know could afford to live there now. It has been, as the British say, tarted up. The chocolate factory, the cannery are fancy malls, destinations full of boutiques, restaurants, tourists. The railroad is long gone. So are all the artists and musicians and writers. Even the bars are much tonier. I don't think there are any neighborhood jam sessions or poetry readings in them. Walking down the street, you don't hear jazz.

I lived on Upland Road in Cambridge in a second-floor apartment of a three-decker. Unfortunately for us, the apartment under us that controlled the heat was occupied by three MIT graduate students who turned it off completely when they went on vacation. The kitchen floor sloped toward the yard and the railroad behind us. If you dropped a radish or an egg, it would roll till it arrived at the far wall. Down the street were two communes and several buildings crammed with students. A trolley took me to Harvard Square, where I could browse in any of twenty-two bookstores. Cheap lunch spots offered Middle Eastern, Greek, Chinese, and comfort food. The rent was cheap, and parking free.

Ten years later, I could still find cheap lodging in Cambridge in a commune. My soon to be husband lived near the Martin

Luther King School in a nice ground floor apartment that rented for $70 a month.

Now I cannot imagine what the rents are, but I know they are amazingly pricey. Many old flats are condos now. Only a few bookstores remain in Harvard Square. There are boutiques, chain stores, many restaurants, some fancy enough to be critiqued by the experts who do that sort of thing. For me it's no longer a destination, and years go by when I haven't had any reason to go there. The changes to Harvard Square make me aware how the importance of writing and books has almost vanished and how much we have become consumers of clothing and restaurant meals.

The transformation of Manhattan's Lower East Side into the East Village is too familiar to need me to discuss it. I would only say that when I lived there, it was cheap and I ate great cheap food and shopped in real markets where barrels of olives, pickles, smoked and brined fish stood among stalls of vegetables brought in from the country.

I lived on the Upper West Side in a six-room, rent-controlled apartment that cost $240 a month. After I had moved to the Cape, I stayed while in town doing a benefit in the same building in an identical apartment three floors down from my old haunt. There were eight people living there to split the rent of $2,500, and then I heard from one of them that it sold for half a million a few years later.

When I moved to the Cape in 1971, my house was built for $25,000 by hippies. There were essentially no building codes. We made our own septic system by digging a huge hole by hand and using cement blocks to line it. One of the guys used to tell me they were stoned all the time they were working on my house. When real plumbers came to fix anything after we moved in, they would fall down giggling.

Still, there were lots of people living here who thrived on almost nothing. Summer people lent their houses generally for nominal or no rent, usually for doing upkeep or chores. In summer, all the folks who had been camping in the houses of summer people would move in together till after Labor Day in some house they pooled their money to rent. I had friends who lived off the land essentially, shellfishing, fishing in the stocked ponds, drying, smoking, freezing what they dug or caught. There were large swaths of uninhabited land where blueberries grew wild as did barberries, blackberries. In the dunes wild cranberries could be found. Abandoned orchards yielded apples and pears. I even found a decent amount of gone-wild asparagus. You could get enough wood to heat your house in the old woodlots.

As still goes on among year-round people, although seldom the newcomers from the suburbs, a lot of barter took place. We volunteered in a food co-op that brought in bulk food, grains, anything dried, potatoes, carrots, whatever we could find. A local fisherman would haul a whole swordfish into the back of the bookstore. A chain of calling would alert us. He'd cut it up, we'd pay him and come home with super-fresh swordfish steaks. We still had working farms here. You could get eggs warm from the hen, fresh-killed chickens and ducks—we cleaned out the chicken coops at one farm every fall for the manure we'd haul away. Radicals had found homes here from the turn of the century until real estate prices soared. Some went underground here during the McCarthy witch hunts.

Much has changed. When the deduction for second homes went into effect, everything began to change. Real estate prices for land and for houses began to soar and have reached ridiculous levels. Many young people, even those born here, have been priced out of town. Woods are cut down for McMansions with great views of each other. No Trespassing signs went up where we had freely walked and picnicked and collected firewood. Farms were chopped into subdivisions. These summer people are not part of the community in any meaningful way. Generally unless something annoys them, they have no interest in local politics or problems. One of them actually said to me, when I was talking about water issues, "Don't tell me! I want to keep this place perfect in my mind."

There used to be mostly year-round people and now there are mostly summer people who own houses. Land was cheap when I moved here. There were ordinary houses that you could buy if you didn't want to build from scratch. Now there are many teardowns. Wealthy people buy perfectly livable houses, tear them down and erect McMansions that they use a couple of months a year.

Now a number of the people who consider themselves year-round residents actually no longer live here year-round. These newcomers are affluent enough to avoid what they don't find pleasant. They don't work here. They go off to San Allende Mexico, to Puerto Rico, to Florida or Arizona or the Caribbean for much of the winter or even longer. Half our friends disappear. They communicate via annoying messages about how warm it is where they are, as if we give a damn. They are gloating. I don't have any desire to go where they are. Winters are sometimes easy, sometimes desperately hard. But I don't like hot weather. (My brain doesn't function above 75°F.) I actually work. Winter is always a great time to get a lot of writing done.

There were folks who lived off the land when first I moved here; nobody does that now. Politics here is always passionate, but then far more inhabitants cared what happened. I have a sense of the history of this place that few of the new people share. This is a not a real place to many of the people who visit or summer here, but how real is it to the folks who disappear for much of the year? I love the land in a very dogged and hardworking way. I am tied to it. My mother and my dead cats are part of the soil. I'd like to end up that way. Living here has made me attuned to the seasons, tides, the moon, the birds and animals who inhabit this land with me. I worry about the future of the Outer Cape that is in danger of becoming a series of ghost towns in the season that used to be the busiest for local people.

Of course now we have a local movie theater that shows four films at once, more and better restaurants, a nice grocery store in town with a gourmet section and grass-fed beef, two live theaters, good vets, doctors who didn't used to treat horses. In some ways life is better. But young people born here mostly can't afford to stay, and your employees may have to live five or six towns away. Our population is far more affluent and much older. My husband says it's a wonderful assisted living community.

Some things are creeping back. After huge fights with relocated suburbanites, more locals are raising chickens and bees again. Once again I can get fresh eggs from naturally raised chickens that live a good life outside when it's reasonable to be there. A few people keep goats once again. We're not the only ones who grow all our own vegetables. But the Outer Cape will never again be the wild and wooly place for people who want to get out of the system and live simply and on little income.

I worry about the future of Wellfleet, with more and more of the land covered with empty houses. There is still poverty, invisible to the summer people. Our food pantry is heavily used. Second-hand clothes are much in fashion for many who live here all the time. Our population ages—so many retirees and those of us who have lived here since it was affordable and a busy village—and who will take care of the infirm and disabled? Labor Day used to be the beginning of our active political meetings and actions. Now some groups have to give up meeting for the winter because so many of their members have abandoned the town for someplace warm. Even the local committee organized around creating year-round jobs went on hiatus because so many of its members are not truly year-round.

I love this place but its future frightens me. Wellfleet is beautiful in all weathers, never more so than during the fiercest of winters. I wish more homeowners could feel that way, could feel a real attachment to the land.

Real estate in cities and in places where people want to vacation has become something priced out of most folks' reach. The rich occupy more and more space, and those without much money are pushed out and pushed out, as once western expansion drove the Native Americans off land that had handily supported them for millennia. Areas mixed racially with a lot of local interaction vanish. Artists move into abandoned industrial buildings and a few years later, they're priced out of the new condos for executives. Neighborhoods get neatened up and we consider this an improvement. Not so sure, myself.

What they call acts of god

How gorgeous is the snow and deadly.
The roads are gone under its drifts.
Hundreds of thousands without power
in a frozen world where the wind
howls like a pack of coywolves.

Already hypothermia fatalities
mount—which is to say, huddling
under blankets the old, the frail,
babies shivered, stopped shivering
and froze to death.

It costs too much to bury over-
head lines, the power company
officials say, who never went
without water, without light
never cowered in the frigid dark:

decisions made by those whom
they do not impact, do not kill.
*We don't believe in climate
change and besides, the cost
benefit ratio does benefit us.*

Drought from agribusiness stealing
water. Lawns green in suburban
desert. Houses washed away from
cheaply done levees. In New Orleans
rebuild for the rich and tourists

and let the Ninth Ward rot into weeds.
Insurance companies hope you'll
grow senile before they pay.
Politicians sit on money to rebuild.
And we call these natural disasters.

STATEMENT ON CENSORSHIP FOR THE PENNSYLVANIA REVIEW

ONE OF THE WORST things about the attack of the Right on the arts is that workers in the arts begin to censor their imaginations or are censored. This dampening effect operates on the local and casual level all of the time now; I know of an accomplished novelist who was dropped from a reading series on Cape Cod in which he had performed successfully because of a sudden concern on the part of the organizer for the sexual content of his works—something no one had thought to question three or four years earlier. If something in a piece of writing is disquieting, the permeating atmosphere does not say to us: *This disturbs me, so I should reexamine my attitudes, beliefs and superstitions to decide if my discomfort is a sign of true offense or my own recalcitrance*; but rather, *This disturbs me and therefore I should not need to experience it*; or even, *This might disturb somebody in the community, and therefore we will exclude that possibility by going with the easy, the sentimental, the obvious, or the academically obscure that bores but never threatens.*

This censorship becomes internalized, because of course every writer wants and needs readers, and words perish if no one can read or hear them. This internalized censorship operates from the level of the first conception of an idea. It operates on subject matter, treatment, imagery, not only on what we will publish or submit, but on what we will permit ourselves to imagine. My best work has often come when I am pushing my own limits, and I suspect that must be true for at least some other writers.

There is another type of censorship which works in tandem with the overt attacks from the religious and moral right. That is the refusal of white male writers to consider the vast majority of others as being of equal weight with themselves. Most men still read few women and few writers of color, whether male or female. They still make their lists with one or two token women. They still give their prizes and grants to each other. Like the censorship of the Right, the censorship of the white males who run most arts organizations, departments of literature and writing, foundations and committees, appears to those exercising this exclusion as just, moral and The Way Things Not Only Are But Ought To Be Forevermore. I have hundreds of male writer Facebook "friends" who would never list any of my works as liked or even read. Probably because they haven't been. When I see "likes" that include a number of women—not necessarily me—I'm delighted.

Thus we find ourselves dealing with censorship without and within the arts community, and often within our own brains. I fear entropic death by Vanilla Pudding. I fear words without passion, stories without lust, publications by the meter and meaning by the centimeter. I fear we will hold back and no more be loftily furious, no more low down dirty and mean, honor verbal stuffing and elevate the production of the bland and tedious and willfully obscure to our dominant art form—as perhaps we already have. Ha Shem speaks out of the whirlwind, not out of the central air conditioning. That still small voice that commands us seldom urges that we eat our gruel and stay respectable and meek. Imperatives from the deep imagination are always to get up and walk out, stand up and be counted, take a long flying leap of chance, open your mouth and roar, descend into the pit, don't just climb the mountain but move it. The art of the present that future generations often find most valuable is that which contemporaries consider awkward in form or content. The muse is rarely polite.

FAME, FORTUNE, AND OTHER TAWDRY ILLUSIONS

MY NAME IS NOT a household word like Drano or Kleenex. I'm probably less famous than the best fly fisherman in the States or the curling champion. Mostly people have no particular reaction when they meet me, although you can never be sure. My former gynecologist "knows who I am" because his receptionist Audrey read one of my novels. However, from time to time people recognize me on the street or in odd and disconcerting circumstances like in a shopping mall when I was trying on a skirt; or another time in a restaurant when Woody and I were having a bloody if moderately quiet argument. I am not so bad about accidental recognition as I used to be. I do not try to crawl into my own pocket or pretend that if I don't move a muscle or breathe, I will wake in my own bed, but I can't say I ever behave more gracefully than a sneak thief caught.

Publishing books, especially about women, brings letters that can break your heart: women losing custody of their children, women defined as crazy because they rebelled against being an unpaid domestic or took a female lover, women in all shapes and colors of trouble.

> Women dyeing the air with desperation,
> women weaving like spiders from the gut
> of emptiness, women
> swollen with emotion, women with words
> piling up in the throat like fallen leaves . . .
> —"Women of letters" (excerpt) from *Early Grrrl*

You also get flattering letters from women as well as some men who tell you what your books have meant to them. You also receive hate mail, if you have any visible politics.

The admirers who do not give pleasure are those who call up, generally when you are sleeping or writing, making supper, entertaining friends, and say, "Hello, I read your book, I happen to be in Wellfleet, and can I come over?" There is no way to satisfy such a caller. When I was younger, I was so astonished and grateful that anybody had read anything of mine and liked it, I would invariably say yes. Dreadful, dreadful scenes resulted. Worse than that, whole boring evenings and days and someone who felt that they had the right to invade again at will and at some point would have to be dealt with forcefully. People who want to invite themselves into your house to meet you generally are pushy and sometimes more than a little nuts, and nothing less than letting them move in or letting them have at least an arm or leg for their own will satiate a baseless hunger. Now I make excuses, unless I know the person in some way, unless a genuine connection exists so that we can hope for two-way communication.

Every week several books and at least one manuscript arrive with requests for blurbs, criticism, help of some sort. I used to try to respond to all those requests, but I got further and further and further behind. The books I now put on a pile in order of when they arrived (I am currently a year and eight months behind) and

the manuscripts I promptly return, if the authors provided post-
age. I do not attempt to read manuscripts at all, unless it is for
someone I know or I have agreed to the request in advance. All
the books I do finally skim at least and a certain number I read,
but I feel snowed in by them. I remember how long I was utterly
unknown. I feel guilty, but I know rationally that if I were to read
even a quarter of them, I would do nothing else. Unlike academics, I don't have long vacations or often any vacations longer than
overnight. To make a living at writing, I have to hustle and work
six days a week.

I travel a lot giving readings, and there the weirdness flour-
ishes in some pockets like mold. People go through ego dances
before me that I find confusing and bemusing. I do not have a
middle-class patina. I like best to talk to people one on one, not
necessarily about me. Women who go about giving readings are
expected to act like ladies, like mommies, or like tough dykes, and
I don't fit into any of those standard roles.

What do people want from somebody they have heard of?
It is not even, frequently, a matter of having read your work and
formed expectations, for I have gone through upsetting pas-de-
deux with individuals who had no idea what kind of work I produce. I was pure celebrity to them. Of the people who have some
familiarity, many are attached to one particular novel and express
resentment that I do not resemble physically or in character Vida
in *Vida*—that I am not a native speaker of Spanish, like Consuelo
in *Woman on the Edge of Time*, or a systems analyst like Miriam
in *Small Changes*, have never been homeless like Mary in *The
Longings of Women* and do not live with a daughter and a stroke-
enfeebled mother like Suzanne in *Three Women*. I have had fans
become hostile when I tried to explain that a novel is not auto-
biographical. The hostility seems to divide into those who feel put

upon (I thought it was true and now I find it's just a story!) and those who suspect you're trying to keep the truth from them; all novels are thinly disguised autobiography and you're just trying to cover up being a lesbian or being a mother who has lost custody of her children, or whatever.

Readers of the poems tend to have somewhat more accurate expectations, although one of the first things always said when I get off the plane is, "I/we expected you to be taller." I intend to write a poem soon about being four feet tall, and then everybody will say, "Oh, but we expected you to be smaller." All microphones are preset as if everybody were five feet ten, and the podiums are sized accordingly.

Once in a while you arrive into a situation where somebody has decided beforehand that you are their sex object. You land and are visited with this great rush that has nothing whatsoever to do with you, and which seems to assume that you have no commitments, no attachments, but are really a figment of their sexual imagination capable of fitting right into the fantasies they have worked up. I find that so off-putting that I don't even feel flattered. Mostly men do this, but sometimes women do it. There may even be the implication that they got you this real nice gig, paying more than they think you or any woman is worth, so you should thank them by rolling over belly-up in bed. That happened a lot more when I was younger, but even at my age, it still happens sometimes.

Sometimes you walk into a situation where the brass of the department didn't want you. You are the sop to the younger faculty or the small contingent of feminists or radicals. I was once introduced in Illinois by the head of the English Department in this way: "Our speaker tonight is Marge Piercy. I never heard of her, but the younger faculty made me invite her." End of introduction.

My advice to the struggling young writer is, never thank anybody sexually, and never use your body as payment or prepayment for help. Fuck only people you want, and then no matter what goes wrong and how you get clobbered emotionally, at least you will have catered to your own sexual tastes. If you are a woman, you have to be especially careful you don't get known as X's girlfriend, because then you can write "The Four Quartets" and still people will say you got published because you were X's girlfriend.

Every writer has some groupies, and how you deal with them is your own decision, within the law. You can sense that a great many of them would not like you as you are, as opposed to the idealized or otherwise fictional image they are toting around; or what they offer is a come-on for expecting that you are going to be for them what Joanna Russ called a magic mommy: solve all their problems, get them published or produced or whatever, make the world right—for them—and have no real needs of your own. Such encounters are programmed for disaster.

Oftentimes women who have achieved some small success find that the man or woman they lived with beforehand cannot adjust to what they view as an unnecessary fuss about somebody they knew back when. Fame loses you lovers and friends, as well as bringing people flocking closer. It does, however, make it easier to find new relationships. You can pick and choose a little. That doesn't mean you'll choose any more intelligently than you did when you were seventeen and still squeezing pimples or twenty-five and invisible as a grain of sand at the seashore, but you may have learned something.

Many men and many women cannot bear success even of the most limited and partial sort coming to someone they married or whose life they have been sharing. They may feel they cannot hold on to their lover with all the new competition, real or imagined.

More often they resent what they feel is the shift of emphasis from themselves as center of the marriage or life, to the other person who was supposed to dance attendance on them, not be rushing off to Paducah to give poetry readings, not be signing books, making speeches, or giving interviews. Certainly they should not be on radio or television or be photographed in the paper grinning, no matter how foolishly.

You will, as a traveling woman, find all too often that a welcoming fuss, however minor, also infuriates local men who feel that you are after all just a cunt and they've seen better, and why isn't everyone fussing about *them*? Similarly you will find as a traveling woman that frequently academic women in universities, who may write a poem or two a year or always meant to write someday, will look at you with annoyance and just about say to you, why all the attention on you? You're just a woman like me. Why should they pay you to come in here and read, lecture, pontificate?

People also commonly confuse three things that are quite distinct. As an American poet you can achieve a certain measure of fame, but you don't get rich and you don't acquire power. The Bush family is rich and the Bush family is powerful. Bill Gates is very rich. Allen Ginsberg may have been famous, but he didn't own half of Bolivia or even New Jersey, and he wasn't consulted on the national defense budget or our policies toward Venezuela. Morris the Cat enjoyed far more fame than any writer I know, but you didn't imagine him wielding power.

Few writers are rich. If they are, maybe they inherited money. When you hear about a $100,000 paperback deal, the hardcover publisher usually takes $50,000, the agent $7,500, and the writer's share on paper is $42,500, except that she got a $15,000 advance to finish the book, so that $15,000 is taken out of her share. That gives her $27,500 minus taxes. Let's say it takes her three years to write a novel, I would think a decent average of what people need. My shortest book took two years; the others, all longer. That gives her about $9,000 a year income for the next three years. Happy $100,000 deal!

For a writer, having some fame is surely better than having none, since if people have heard of you they are likelier to buy your books than if they have not, or at least to take them out of the library; but it doesn't mean you're drinking champagne out of crystal goblets while you count your oil revenue shares, and it doesn't mean you have any choice about how the world is run. Similarly the writer above with the $9,000 coming in for the next three years is immensely better off than she was when she wrote for an occasional $5 or $50 fee from the quarterlies, or when she did a reading a week for twenty weeks at one hundred bucks per reading, ending up sick in bed and worn out with no writing done and having earned a total of $2,000 after her expenses on the road are deducted.

Make no mistake: I like applause. I adore being admired. I even like signing books, which I understand some writers don't. I'm tickled somebody is buying them. I work hard when I give workshops and try to give honest and useful answers when students question me. I like having my books discussed; I passionately care to have them read. I even like giving workshops where I read lots of often incoherent or sloppy student writing—I do enjoy trying to teach them how to make it all better.

But I resent jealousy, especially when beamed at me by people who have made as clear choices in their lives as I have. I know how invisible I was to the kind of people I meet around universities and other institutions in my nonfamous life, when I was poor and subsisting on various underpaid part-time positions.

I know how they treat their secretaries, waitresses, cleaning women, store clerks. I was living in a slum, eating macaroni and wearing second-hand clothes (not then fashionable) and chewing aspirins because I couldn't pay a dentist while I wrote the first six novels before the one that got published. I can never forget how little respect or understanding I received from other people when I was a serious but largely unpublished writer, not sanctified by the fame machine. It's hard getting started in the arts, and one of the things that is the hardest, is that nobody regards you as doing real work until somebody certifies you by buying what you do.

Another kind of irritation I provoke in resident or visiting male writers is drawing larger audiences or selling more books than they do, whereupon they are careful to inform me that it's because I "jumped on this women's lib bandwagon." I'm fashionable, but they're universal. Universal includes only white men with university degrees who identify with patriarchal values, but never mind that. If they imagine it helps me to be known as a feminist or a lefty, they have never read my reviews. The overwhelming majority are by reviewers who hate the politics and who feel none of the obligations I feel when I review works to identify my bias and try to deal with the writer's intentions. Jealous males also seem to have failed to notice that feminists no longer have access to the media and enjoy no political clout. To try to bring about social change in this country is always to bring down punishment on your head. My grandfather, a union organizer, was murdered. At various times in my life I have had my phone tapped, been tailed, been beaten very, very thoroughly, gassed, had my mail opened, lost jobs, been vetoed as a speaker by boards of trustees in Utah, been heckled, insulted, dismissed, refused grants and positions that have consistently gone to lesser writers; and yet they imagine there is some bandwagon I am riding on. A tumbril, perhaps.

Then there are local politicos. A phenomenon I have noticed since my antiwar days is how the rank-and-file in American movements for social change treat those who have assumed, perhaps fought for or perhaps had thrust upon them, some kind of leadership. Frequently the mistrust with which your own treat you is sufficient to send people into paranoia or early burn-out, away from political activity damned fast; it certainly contributes to crossing over to the Establishment where at least you can expect that people will be polite to you.

If you are effective at anything, you will be sharply criticized. The real heroes of many people on the Left and in the women's community are failures who remain pure according to a scriptural line and speak only to one another. Also lefties may harbor fantasies that you are rich. At every college a feminist will demand to know how I dare publish with New York houses rather than the local Three Queer Sisters Press—as if the point of feminism isn't to try to reach women who don't agree already, rather than cozily assuming that we are a "community" of pure souls and need only address one another. Often women who have some other source of support (husband, family, trust fund, academic job) will accuse you of selling out if you get paid for your writing or for speaking.

Feminist presses have an important function, as do all small presses. With the New York publishers owned by large conglomerates, small presses are the one hope for freedom of expression and opinion. The all-pervasive electronic media are not open to those of us who do not share the opinions of the board of directors of Exxon-Mobil. What was true in the days of Thomas Paine and true today is that you can print your own pamphlet or book. The printed word is far more democratic than television. You do not need to be a millionaire to acquire and run a publishing enterprise. My partner Ira Wood and I ran a small press for ten years that published many serious writers who could no longer get published in New York—until we couldn't afford to run it any longer. Many important writers were first published by small presses, and some such as James Joyce were published by small presses for their whole professional lives.

Fame has a two-edged effect on the character. On the one hand, if you suffer from early self-hatred, then fame can mellow you. If you like yourself, you may be able to like others better. Naturally I apply this to myself, believing myself easier-going since the world has done something besides kick me repeatedly in the breadbasket. However, I would also say that fame—like money and probably like power—is habituating. You become so easily accustomed to being admired, that you begin to assume there is something inherently admirable in your character and person, a halo of special soul stuff that everybody ought to recognize at first glance.

Fame can oil the way to arrogance. It can easily soften you to cozy mental flab, so you begin to believe that every word you utter is equally sterling and every word you write is golden. There is a sort of balloon quality to some famous men—including famous writers—and you know that they may never actually sit alone in a room agonizing and working as hard as it takes to do good work, ever again. You may even come to regard yourself as inherently lovable, which is peculiar, given how writers actually spend a lot of time recording the bitter side of the human psyche. Having a fuss made over one leads to the desire to have more of a fuss made over one, and even to feel that nobody else quite so much deserves being fussed over, or that any fuss, any award, any prize, is only a tiny part of what one truly deserves.

We can easily confuse the luck of the dice and the peculiarities of remuneration in this society with inner worth. I recently overheard an engineer who writes occasional poetry berating the organizer of a reading because he felt he wasn't being given a prominent enough spot in the line-up. "My time is worth something," I heard him announce, and he meant it: he considered that what he was paid as an engineering consultant carried over to his poetry, which meant that his poetry was more to be valued, since the time he spent writing it was worth more an hour than the time of other poets.

Once in a women's workshop at a writers' conference, several of the mothers were talking about feeling guilty about the time they took to write, time taken from their children. I asked one woman who had published two novels if being paid for her work didn't lessen her guilt, and she agreed. Finally the group decided that if enough people seem to value your work, whether by paying for it or just by paying attention to it, then you would feel less guilt. You could begin to justify demanding from the others in your life the time and space to write. Certainly attention paid to your work seems to validate your effort and makes it easier to protect the time necessary to accomplish something.

I suppose the ultimate problem with the weirdness I encounter on the road is that it makes me wary. It's hard to respond to people I meet sometimes, when I am not at all sure what monsters are about to bulge up from under the floorboards. I also find demands that I provide instant intimacy, or that I should walk into rooms ready to answer probing questions about my life and my loves, to be patently absurd. The books are public. But I am not my books. I don't believe that people who have bought or read the books have a right therefore to sink their teeth in my arm. I had an unpleasant experience at a fancy Catholic school recently where a group of women made demands on me that I found silly. I gave a good reading, worked hard to make the workshop useful, went over their work. Then I was attacked because I was not "open emotionally." One of them quoted to me a phrase of mine from "Living in the Open," which apparently meant to her that you must "love" everybody you meet and gush on command.

For some people, admiration of something you have done easily converts into resentment—disappointment that you are not Superwoman with a Madonna smile, or resentment if you do not bear obvious scars. They can forgive accomplishment if the woman who arrives is an alcoholic, suicidal, miserable in some overt way. To be an ordinary person with an ordinary life of ups and downs and ins and outs is not acceptable.

Admiration can sour into hatred. Bigger celebrities inspire it far more than us small fry, for which I am thankful, but I would rather not inspire it at all. You meet an occasional person who, if you do not work a miracle—light up their life, change things, take one look at them and say, Yes, you are the one—they feel that they have been failed in some way.

If what people want from me is a good energizing reading, a useful workshop, an honest lecture, answering questions as carefully and fully as I can, then they are satisfied. If what they want is a love affair with a visiting Mother Goddess, a laying on of hands to make them real, a feeding of soul hungers from a mystical breast milk fountain, then they are doomed to disappointment. For that act, I charge a whole lot more.

HOUSEWIVES WITHOUT HOUSES

THINK OF A HOMELESS person. What comes to mind is a man, probably middle-aged and ragged, a man alone, without family or social ties, perhaps an ex–mental patient or someone with a drug or alcohol problem. Certainly a walk through the streets of our cities will strengthen this stereotype.

The female counterpart is the bag lady. She is layered in old clothes, pushing a grocery cart or dragging her overloaded shopping bags. As she shuffles along, she mutters to herself. She crouches in the doorway of a shop in the early morning, not yet ousted from her refuge; she squats in a local park.

I can identify the moment I became aware that these visible homeless who populate the insufficient shelters are only part of the story. As a poet, I travel a lot giving readings and workshops on college campuses and in cities. On a Midwestern campus where I was in brief residence, I met a woman of forty who was living on campus and in faculty homes—uninvited. This was a small town where houses were not locked up and burglar-alarmed. She kept an eye on the professors' comings and goings, so she could enter their houses through windows and stay there. She also lived in university buildings. It was my need to find quiet time to work on a novel that caused me to discover her. Once she realized I had no intention of reporting her, she became friendly.

In Santa Monica I noticed that every rhododendron, every bush in the plantings around the waterfront hotels and in the beachfront park, all housed someone for the night. The hotels would turn on their watering system at six a.m. to clear them out. I had gone to buy yogurt in a convenience store. The man ahead of me was mouthing off about the homeless, how disgraceful they are, how shameless, how they were bringing down the property values. The man at the cash register was fidgeting. Finally he said, "We're not shameless. A lot of us have jobs, but we don't make enough to afford housing. I work, I pay taxes just like you."

Far from being a lone wolf, this man had a wide web of relatives and friends. He never slept on the street. He spent two or three days with each of his acquaintances, bringing his sleeping bag, bringing food so he would not freeload. It took him six to seven weeks to make his circuit, and then he began again. Being homeless required planning and the ability to get along with all sorts of people and never to wear out his welcome.

In my novel *The Longings of Women*, one of the protagonists is a homeless woman of sixty-one, Mary Burke, who was a mother and homemaker married to a Washington bureaucrat. After divorce, she slowly spiraled downward economically, until she was homeless. When I was researching the novel, I became accomplished at recognizing homeless women in malls and managing to engage them. Malls are ideal places for finding the invisibly homeless, the ones who can pass, the ones who pretend to be like everyone else. Unlike the sociological studies of women in shelters I had read, almost every one of these women had been married.

These are not women who talk to themselves, who wear obvious old clothes in grungy and unwashed layers. They can pass for middle-class women, and their survival depends on their ability to do that. Many work at part-time or minimum-wage jobs and cannot manage high rents and huge deposits for rent and utilities.

I have become sensitive to cars that are dwellings, and I see them everyplace in the cities, sometimes occupied by men, sometimes by women, sometimes by whole families. Where I live on Cape Cod, I see them too. I can tell the difference between tourists who are saving the price of a motel for the night and homeless people who camp in the woods or in their cars. It is the way the car is set up for living. Someone who lives in a car cannot be neat but must make efficient use of space. Their bedding, their clothes, their food scene occupy the car, often with some sort of window coverings.

Although our expectations of what women are like have certainly changed, in many ways we still identify women with home. James Thurber's cartoon of the house as a crouching woman still fits many people's stereotypes. Some homeless women I met had been housewives, but the house had been lost with the marriage. A surprising number had children. They showed me their pictures. The children could not take them in, would not, were in trouble themselves. Maybe the husband or wife disliked the mother and would not open the home to them. That was not an aspect of their lives they wanted to discuss.

Almost all fantasized about a better job that would pay enough for a studio apartment, a room, someplace of their own. The most depressing part of these conversations was how normal these women seemed. A few, who had spent time on the streets, told me that living so vulnerably made women crazy. But these women could have been my neighbors, my friends. Dropped in a functioning family again, they would carry on seamlessly.

Middle-class life, which my parents spent their lives aspiring to, used to seem solid and secure. If you worked for a company, and if you weren't a hopeless drunk or mechanical idiot, you could expect to have that job till you retired. If you got married, you expected to stay married. You thought you knew where you were going to be in forty years. This stability is gone. These women are the victims of economic choices and changes they have no purchase on. Incessantly they wonder what they did wrong. A dozen experts would give them a dozen answers. But when I was talking with them, one thought kept occurring: this could be anybody. This could be me.

Homelessness is not solely an American problem. The British have had squatters for years. The first homeless I ever saw abroad (I was familiar with hoboes in Detroit) were the *clochards* of Paris, men and women who slept under the bridges on the Seine. South American cities are often surrounded by wastelands of improvised shantytowns. In Cairo, the mausoleums have become cities of the living who lack better housing. In India countless people live in the streets. But we are not accustomed to considering this a reasonable outcome for lives of hard work, whether in paid jobs or unpaid homemaking. A real program for displaced homemakers would certainly offer help to these women before they slip onto the streets.

In recent years, I have encountered more and more families with children living in their cars or wherever they can shelter, using what facilities they can to stay clean, looking and looking for work. The children were usually in school but of course their lives were hardly normal and they must never let the school find out they did not actually live in some abode in the district. Homelessness is not a disease or a pathology. It is a result of our lack of affordable housing and lack of jobs that can support at least minimal comfort and security.

The hows; there is no why

Friday go to any lost & found:
ask for brown gloves medium.
Even if they don't fit so good,
they'll keep your hands warm.

Go to another and ask for a plaid
scarf. That almost always works.
If you order tea take out the tea
bag at once, put in ketchup

and mustard. Makes sort of soup.
Go to department teas at colleges.
Astronomy this week, psychology
next. Eat up on cookies, coffee

always with lots of milk or cream
and sugar. Keep refilling. Dump-
ster diving is requisite but be careful.
If you smell, you label yourself.

Upscale food stores often put out
samples of cheese, spreads, fruit.
If they're unattended, you can
go back again and again.

In the glut of superabundance
linger and watch. Keep up
appearances, blend in as best
you can and you may survive.

At least a while. Mice, roaches
live on people's crumbs as do
the invisible homeless slipping
like grey fog through any street.

"LIVING OFF THE GRID"
Marge Piercy interviewed by Terry Bisson

Cape Cod? Isn't that a weird, or at least rather sandy, place for a writer to live?

Not at all. There is a long history of writers, painters and radicals living on the Outer Cape. I don't understand what sandy has to do with it. We grow just about all our own vegetables, our own fruit, many perennials, a garden of organically grown roses, all in the soil you seem to scorn. It's a fecund place.

When I moved here, at a time when in part due to Cointelpro, the movement in NYC was destroying itself. This was a very cheap place to live. I've written about that in an essay in this volume, "Gentrification and Its Discontents." My house was built for $25,000 by a bunch of stoned hippies. When I moved here, there were many people living off the grid. Several Communists had spent their underground years during the McCarthy era on the Outer Cape. It's still viewed as the wild and woolly boondocks by people who live in the more suburban parts of the mid-Cape and upper Cape.

The last decade or so, we've been inundated by wealthy summer people between July 4 and Labor Day, and now many suburban types with money have retired here; but there are still remnants of how we lived then. There's still a barter economy that's important to us, and a lot of writers and artists still live and work here—fewer in Provincetown than there used to be, as it's turned way too expensive—but just as many in Wellfleet.

The Outer Cape is very liberal politically, and most residents are ecologically oriented. There's a tradition of acceptance of all kinds of lifestyles and orientations. Gays and lesbians were comfortable here for probably a century before that was true on the mainland. Black sea captains operated out of the Cape while slavery was still legal.

You have not only consistently published poetry but gained a wide circle of readers who are not poets themselves. That puts you in rare company. What do you think of Edna St. Vincent Millay? E.E. Cummings? Gary Snyder?

I admire Gary Snyder and his ecological commitment very much. Edna St. Vincent Millay was outspoken and feisty. I admire E.E. Cummings's musicality, less for his visual-only poems, not at all for his occasional anti-Semitism.

What does the current state of Detroit mean to you?

That the money and whites fled. That those who made their money out of the labor of hard workers did not give a damn what happened to them. That great music and writing and all kinds of art can still come from a place that is dear to me. That it is possible for Detroit to survive with new ideas but it will be difficult. Growing up in Detroit prepared me to be a lefty and a feminist.

I wasn't white when I grew up. Jews and Blacks were always lumped together in racist and anti-Semitic propaganda handed out by the Silver Shirts on street corners and pumped over the radio by Father Coughlin. The neighborhoods with housing bans (most of Detroit) made no distinction between us.

Even though you are a bona-fide New York Times *bestseller, you describe yourself (in your memoir* Sleeping with Cats, *I think) as a midlist writer. Is that humility or pride?*

I never made the kind of money bestsellers do, and because I am a midlist writer, I can no longer get my fiction published in New York. My poetry does well enough to still get published by Knopf. I'm too old, too left, and too feminist to be a true bestseller author or to be interesting to the young Ivy League trust fund people who are most of the New York editors today. One of the reasons we started and ran Leapfrog Press for ten years, until we could no longer afford to continue, was to publish other serious midlist writers who could no longer find editors in New York houses—of which there are fewer and fewer. Those that remain are like other corporations that produce face creams and detergents. There's little pretense they're doing more than watching the bottom line.

The demise of midlist writers is self-fulfilling. The few New York publishers left put all their effort into a few titles. The rest of the list has to do their own publicity, if they can, and hope that the occasional reviews that still exist help. Then when you come along with your next book, all they look at is how many copies the last one sold.

Dystopias are easy. You are one of the few writers who tackle serious utopias. What are the rewards of that endeavor?

Science fiction, speculative fiction, whatever you want to call it, is one of the ways to explore social issues in fiction. You can explore what it's going to be like if current trends continue. You can change a variable and see what that does.

Dystopias are not as easy as you seem to think. In *Woman on the Edge of Time* and *He, She and It*, I tackle both types. I think *He, She and It* is more relevant today because what I describe in it is happening and happening rapidly. But the reason for writing utopias is to provide a positive image of what can be worked toward, instead of fighting for more of the same, more McDonalds, bigger McMansions, more powerful SUVs, yet more media, cheaper plastic surgery, more deadly and more automated weapon systems. Utopias offer the writer's imaginative portrait of how things might be if we make it so.

What's a worming?

It's a group criticism/self-criticism session familiar to anyone who has read *Fanshen* or anybody who was active in New Left groups toward the later 1960s.

In the utopian vision of Woman on the Edge of Time, *there are no cities, or at least no Big Cities. What happened to the girl who wanted to eat New York?*

I lived in NYC twice, the last time for seven years. What I saw was not delightful: the increasing ownership of the city by the ruling class, the poor and finally also the middle class being pushed out, terrifying police work (believe me, the Red Squad were no philanthropists), real estate prices from hell. Pollution. Being right next to an aging nuclear power plant—but so are we here on the Cape, with no way to evacuate when the local Fukushima clone blows.

I lived in many cities for the first half of my life—Detroit, Chicago, Paris, Boston, San Francisco, Brooklyn, and Manhattan. My lungs were weakened by years of smoking and breathing pollution. I was gassed several times in antiwar demonstrations. By the time I moved to Cape Cod, my lungs were seriously damaged and I was sick. My lungs cleared here.

You have a distinct poetic style combining (for me) the easy lope of Whitman with the taut line of Dickinson. Can you say something about contemporary poets who have influenced you?

You named the poets who influenced me just when I was beginning to write poetry at fifteen. Influence is a matter of adolescence and early adulthood. I'd say the other major influences in late adolescence were Muriel Rukeyser and William Butler Yeats. Muriel was very important to me, as a writer who wrote honestly, passionately, and well about being a woman, as a writer with politics, as a writer whose work was written to be said aloud.

After going through college and learning that proper poetry had to be composed of sestinas written about works viewed in the Uffizi in Florence on a Guggenheim, I dared to go back to writing in my own voice and about my own life after hearing Ginsberg read—but I've included an essay about that in this volume. Needless to say, although I tried numerous times for Guggenheims—for instance to do research for *Gone to Soldiers* and for *He, She and It*—I have received extremely few grants or any free money in my life. I've worked since I was twelve, and what money I have I've made from working for it.

Was your great-grandfather really a pirate?

Great-great-grandfather. I have no idea. My mother told me that about my father's father's father's father, but my mother loved drama and was leery of the Piercys. I know little about my father's family other than that the men went to sea a lot. I saw a memorial to a Piercy captain in the cathedral in Kent.

I know far more about my mother's family and my grand-father on that side, who was a radical and was murdered by the Pinkertons for unionizing the bakery workers in Cleveland. I know about my great-grandfather who was a rabbi in a *stetl* in Lithuania and finally married my grandmother and grandfather when he was fleeing the Czar's police after an unsuccessful revolutionary attempt. I was very close to my maternal grandmother, whom I've written about in my memoir *Sleeping with Cats*. She gave me my religious education, gave me a strong sense of female-based Judaism, told me tales from the *stetl* and from her own difficult and hazardous life. Magic realism? She was a master of tales infused with that.

You got started as a writer pretty early. Or would you call it late?

When I was fifteen, we moved from a small asbestos shack where I slept first in my parents' bedroom and then in a room that was for storage and a passageway, to a much larger house where I had a room of my own upstairs, away from my parents although across the hall from boarders. The bathroom I could use was downstairs and my room was tiny and unheated, but I loved it and began to write seriously in an attempt to deal with contradictions in my life and assorted traumas. A girlfriend I was close to died of a heroin overdose that year, my sweet cat was poisoned by my next-door boyfriend because our little house was sold to an African-American family—the neighborhood was predominantly Black but segregated by blocks. I had gone to school with Blacks and played with them since I was little, so it was hard for me to understand our neighbors' fury. Of course their kids went to a parochial school that was all white.

After my beloved and loving grandmother died, I revolted against Orthodoxy starting with my anger at the rabbi at her funeral. Nothing in my life or around me was the way it was supposed to be according to TV, according to school, according to the propaganda everywhere about America. I had been in a sort of proto-gang where I felt accepted—until we moved. I had been sexually active early but stopped when we moved, as the girls in this new neighborhood were "good girls." I felt like a different animal than those around me. I had already developed some left politics, called myself a socialist. I did not fit in anyplace I could see. I started writing both fiction and poetry. I wrote much better poetry than fiction for a long time. But it all started in a desperate attempt to understand myself and my life and Detroit around me.

You went to Cuba back in the 1960s. What was that like? Do you think of yourself as a socialist today?

I was invited by the Cuban government to spend the summer in Cuba in 1968. It was a very vital time. The blockade had not stifled the economy that much and the arts were free and percolating. I was one of the founders of the North American Congress on Latin America—NACLA—one of the only New Left groups still active today. I subscribe to their newsletter, one of the best sources of information on what's really going on south of the border. I had friendly relations with the Cuban delegation to the UN. That was why I was invited.

I spent the first month trying to explain the New Left to party people and seeing all the official sights. Then I was turned loose. I traveled around Cuba freely, met amazing dancers, painters, filmmakers, poets, all kinds of men and women who'd fought in the revolution, and peasants in the countryside. I argued with party members about sex roles and freedom for sexual orientations, but loved a lot of what I saw and experienced. Cuba is very beautiful and there are lots of pristine wild places still, amazing bird, reptile, crustacean, mammal life. I like Cuban food.

In New York, life was edgy. I received death threats with some regularity from right-wing groups. I'd been beaten in demonstrations. I had been under surveillance in New York—mail cover, at one point a live tap on my apartment, and strange guys in the basement of the apartment house. The men who worked in that building were from the Dominican Republic; they resented the American invasion there and were sympathetic to me and my politics. Plus, I spoke Spanish fluently then and used it every day with them and in the neighborhood. They always warned me about surveillance. If I ever doubted, Ira found proof years later, after I had moved to Cape Cod.*

I had a huge old-fashioned desk I used till I got my first PC in 1982. The desk was not a good place to work on a computer, so Woody built a new desk for me. The old desk had to be broken up to be burned. As Woody was prying it apart, he found an electronic bug on the bottom of one of the drawers. A tiny mike and wires leading away.

Yes, I'm a socialist-anarchist-feminist.

---

* Her partner Ira Wood, a.k.a. Woody.

Is Vida *based on anyone real?*

I knew a lot of the people in the Weather Underground and kept in touch with them. Three of them are still close friends. The character Vida was not based on any particular individual or individuals. I don't work that way. I did not agree with about half of their politics at that time, but I am loyal to friends. And I was proud of how so many of them ran rings around the FBI. *Vida's* still one of the most accurate portrayals of life underground, what led to it, and how the people survived.

You teach a lot, and you and Ira Wood have written a how-to book on writing. Yet in a poem you say that all one can learn is someone else's mannerisms. So which is it?

I don't actually teach a lot. I give a lot of readings, some speeches and three or four workshops a year. I've taught in college on three occasions, two of them for just a quarter or a semester. I did my best, but I was out of my element in academia.

Woody and I both teach craft workshops. You can teach craft. Beyond that, it's pretty much bullshit. If you take four writing workshops, you'll hear four opinions, four definitions of excellent, four sets of instructions and recommendations for writing. The worst workshops are given by people who only write books about how to write but pretty much can't do it themselves. The best way, we always say, to learn to write memoirs is to read memoirs and learn from those that don't work for you as well as from those who do. Look at how they did things. Separate out the craft elements. If you want to write detective stories, read them. If you want to write historical novels, read them.

You seem to share Rexroth's old-fashioned idea that the poet has a public and political, as well a personal artistic, responsibility. How would you describe that responsibility today?

The idea that poetry should be devoid of politics is a modern heresy designed to diminish any slight power we might have, to render us irrelevant. It is a notion that poets before about 1940 would have found really weird. Shakespeare's plays are rife with politics; same with Milton, Dryden, Pope, Wordsworth, Shelley, Byron, and that's only a few British poets. All the Irish poets had political ideas. Go back to the Romans. Find one without politics!

Poets and novelists and memoirists and essayists are all citizens like your plumber or neighborhood cop or clergy. If you don't take an interest, politics may come down on your head, may take away your livelihood, pollute your air, give you cancer from the food you eat, teach your children garbage and false history, make you pay for wars you don't believe in and actually hate.

Do you have a different strategy for writing poetry and fiction? A different schedule? A different desk in front of a different window?

Ideas for novels can't be mistaken for ideas for poems and vice versa. I do both usually all the time but seldom on the same day. I can write prose for a lot longer duration than I can poetry, which is much more intense and concentrated.

You once compared talent to phlogiston. Was that a compliment?

Phlogiston is the substance that the scientists and philosophers of an earlier time used to explain fire. So it stands for any invented thingie that people label the cause of a phenomenon they don't understand.

I read Dance the Eagle to Sleep *when there actually were rebels fighting underground in the USA. If you were writing it today would the protagonists still be teens?*

No, they'd probably be sixty-five-year-old women.

Like me, you were drawn to SDS even though a bit too old. Out of school. Was that a problem?

I joined SDS after searching around to find a group opposing the war in Vietnam that I could agree with. I was a premature antiwar activist, from about 1962 on, before we had officially entered the war. I had a friend who spent time in Vietnam and wrote letters about what was really going on. I had trouble finding anybody else who cared for some time.

I went to one of the big rallies in Washington in 1965 and joined SDS then. I organized off campus in Brooklyn from 1965 on. I worked for *Viet Report* and tried various ways of relating. Then we started NACLA and I was fully involved there. I did power structure analysis and created and ran a database on power structure, the CIA, interlocking directorates among the ruling class, etc. I was recruited into the regional office of SDS because I was one of the few people around who had any experience organizing off campus. I had done some in civil rights and local politics. I was a precinct captain in Chicago during the Kennedy election.

Nobody thought I was much older. I've always looked younger than I am, still do. I was in an open relationship and had many relationships in the Movement. Bob Gottlieb and I started Movement for the Democratic Society to do off-campus organizing after Progressive Labor launched a coup and took over the regional office of SDS. We had teachers, social workers, city planner groups, affinity groups like the Motherfuckers (primarily a motorcycle gang), street theater, buying co-op, child care, etc.

What kind of car do you drive? (I ask this of everyone.)

When I drive at all, it's an old stick shift Volvo. Mostly Woody does the driving, in a truck with four-wheel drive, a Toyota. Most year-rounders here on the Cape drive trucks.

Do you read poetry for fun? Who?

Martín Espada, Dorianne Laux, Joy Harjo, Laura Kasischke, Wisława Szymborska, Tony Hoagland, Philip Levine, Adrienne Rich, Rita Dove, Lucille Clifton, Yehuda Amichai, Paul Celan, Kevin Young, Leslea Newman, Nelly Sachs, Maxine Kumin, Audre Lorde.

One might say all novels are historical. But City of Darkness, City of Light *and* Gone to Soldiers *definitely are. Can you say something about how research informs your work? What about other novelists (thinking in particular of James Jones and Hilary Mantel)?*

Generally I've done a lot of research on the period before I begin work. I work on characters then for some time before I write. After first draft, I know what I need to research and generally do a lot of it all the way through to final draft. The research for

Gone to Soldiers was seven times longer than the novel. For *Sex Wars* (my most recent novel), my research came to 1,900 pages.

What interests me in history is how those periods influenced the present. In *Sex Wars*, one of the alarming aspects is that in the period after the Civil War they were dealing with the same problems and issues we are dealing with today: the rights of women and minorities, immigration, abortion, contraception, income inequality, prison reform, election manipulation.

Bernard Cornwell does excellent research for his novels.

If you had to abandon fiction or poetry, which would it be?

No contest: poetry would win. You can write poetry in a jail cell. If you have no paper, you can memorize your poems. You can say a poem in front of a firing squad. Poetry is highly portable. Novels are not. These days I'm inclining more toward short stories than novels. As I get older, I like shorter forms better than longer ones.

But poetry will always win out. I also make more money these days from my poetry—readings and advances—than from fiction or other prose.

TOUCHED BY GINSBERG AT A (RELATIVELY) TENDER AGE

THIS PIECE IS MOSTLY about Allen Ginsberg's effect on me, since I did not know him personally. As a child, I had written occasional verse, not often and frankly not demonstrating much in the way of talent. It was the kind of stuff bright children write, sing-song rimes about the weather or my cat.

I began to write poetry regularly and passionately when I was fifteen. My grandmother, to whom I was very close and who gave me unrestricted, unconditional love and taught me storytelling and a strongly female Judaism, died of stomach cancer. My beloved cat was poisoned by the boy next door. My girlfriend died of a heroin overdose. We moved from the stone working-class predominantly African-American neighborhood where we had lived since I was two, to a more respectable lower middle-class area of Detroit. I dropped out of the gang that had given me my social identity and stability—I was no longer in that neighborhood or that milieu. Out of my confusion and anger and grief I began to write poetry as well as to read a great deal of it. I started with Whitman and Dickinson, where American prosody began. I passed on to the Romantics, particularly Shelley. By my senior year in high school, I was reading T.S. Eliot, Muriel Rukeyser,

Edward Arlington Robinson, Yeats, H.D. and Baudelaire in translation. I was also reading Marx, Freud and *The Golden Bough*.

Poetry was a way of keeping myself relatively sane and trying to make sense of the world I inhabited, which did not correspond to the world shown on the television we acquired the year we moved or the world that textbooks and school commended to us. The place I had grown up in was far more violent. Radical politics made sense to me. I imitated whatever I read, but I also wrote poems in my own voice and out of my life and my experiences. It was raw, it was choppy. Sometimes it wasn't half bad and sometimes it was god-awful.

When I went off to the University of Michigan, the first person in my family to go to college, I learned that I was not allowed to write poetry like mine. My first boyfriend was a poet trained in classical forms, who politely explained to me that what I wrote was not really poetry, even though my freshman year I was the only poet my age invited to read at a festival and I won a contest. By the time he got done explaining how incorrect I was, and I had been subjected to scorn by the professor of English to whom I had shown my work, I was inhibited. I did not write a poem for a year and a half. When I began again, I won a Hopwood award in my junior year.

What was admired and taught was extremely studied rimed poetry, usually in forms like villanelles, sonnets and other types more suited to Romance languages than to English. I wrote the crabbed intricate pieces I forced myself into like the girdles women were expected to wear then. I was told repeatedly that I could not write about what I cared about. Political poetry was uncouth and not real poetry—I had written reams of it in high school. Also uncouth and unreal was anything having to do with the body as it existed in reality and my experiences as a woman or a Jew. Everything was to be tidy, male, "universal." The most admired pieces seemed to be sonnets about paintings viewed in the Uffizi while abroad on Guggenheims.

I won a major Hopwood in my senior year, money I used to finance a trip to Europe. I spent time in France, Italy, and the Netherlands. I looked at paintings and architecture, practiced my French and Spanish, learned to eat artichokes and drink decent wine, and discovered how thoroughly and profoundly I was both Jewish and American.

I was dissatisfied with my poetry but stuck in the rigid forms and the dry ironic stance I had learned in college. I took my MA at Northwestern and then fled graduate school because my brain was drying up. I was working as a secretary in Chicago when I went with a friend to hear Allen Ginsberg read.

I had vaguely heard of the Beats and was curious. I was also hungry for writing and writers. I had joined a group of African-American and white writers who met weekly and critiqued one another's work and hung out together, but I still felt isolated—from myself as well as from writing in general.

That night Allen Ginsberg broke open the world of writing for me. He wrote in the vernacular. This was real language, living and passionate. He wrote out of his own sexuality, not the way he had been programmed to believe it should be, but as he experienced it in his body and mind. He wrote with emotion and sometimes with humor. His poems were those of a Jew and a radical. As I sat there almost bolting out of my seat, he peeled off me all the veneer of graduate school. I was better educated than I had been before university, certainly, with a wider vocabulary and a sense of the literature that had come before me. I had read widely and critically in English, American, and Irish literatures. But I had lost my voice and my identity as a poet, and hearing him showed me the way back. Because he was writing honestly, he offered to all of us a poetic license to tell our own truths.

Politics and class-consciousness came charging back into my poetry. My own identity as a woman, my background as a working-class Jew from center city Detroit raised in an African-American neighborhood, my involvement in civil rights; my identity as a street kid who loved her grandma, as a woman who was sexually experienced at age eleven and proud of her own sexuality—all that came charging out of the closet. I realized that the strange clumsy feeling I'd had when I was writing in recent years was because I was writing other people's poems, and not my own. My life was not like those of the few privileged women whose poetry we were given, allowed although not excessively encouraged to read. I no longer tried to bleach my expressions or cram my words into straightjackets of ornate rime schemes.

Margaret Atwood in a blurb once called my poems "hairy"— well, that was the night the hair started to grow. I identified with the mixture of seriousness and humor in Ginsberg's poems. They reminded me of stories told by my mother and my grandmother. His work reminded me of nights with my pinochle-playing aunts and uncles when they would tell terrible stories that were also funny. That mix of grimness and pain and humor runs right through my childhood and came back out in my poetry, set free from its ghetto of repression. I would not again attempt to write like an English gentleman professor.

I carried *Howl* with me to Ann Arbor when I went back to visit friends still in graduate school; they thought I had taken leave of my senses. Allen Ginsberg was not to be taken seriously. I had taken leave of the strictures forced upon me as appropriate and proper. I was freed to honesty, to make what I could out of my own politics, my own pain and joy, my working-class background, my sexuality, my Jewishness, my woman's life. I was free to work my way toward my own poetic voice, finally—the voice I had begun with but abandoned—free to write about what had happened to me, what I saw, what I felt, what I thought—in poetry.

The academics may make a fuss about Ginsberg now that he is safely dead and it is fifty years since *Howl* broke a hole in the wall that had been erected around real poetry with the capacity to move people. If you look now at the winners of prestigious prizes, once again too often they write extremely safe poetry, poetry that would never excite anyone, never anger anyone, never give voice to something powerful and inchoate inside that might emerge in words able to bring it into the light. What is dull, ornate and chilly, preferably reasonably oblique, not to say obtuse, is much admired, as it was before Ginsberg knocked the door down and let so many of us out where we could begin to do real work.

Although I happened once or twice to be in the same place as he was, I never met him personally. That does not diminish my gratitude.

TABULA RASA WITH BOOBS

I APPROACH MARILYN MONROE but find it boring in advance, like circling an exotic dump of fifties paraphernalia: Freudian texts, merry widows, brassieres built like rocket launchers, spike heels four inches high the fashion industry is still pushing, shadows of back alley abortions you tell no one about, faded photos of marriage as the holy grail. Marilyn Monroe can be approached as Norma Jeane, the woman who (as her neighbor in bungalow 31, Simone Signoret, said) took three hours to turn herself into "Marilyn." Her work can be critiqued cinematically, with an appreciation of her underrated work as a comic actress—always denigrated not for her beauty, which was taken for granted, but for her talent. She can be treated as an icon, what she presented on the screen and in her life as people imagined it, and what was read into that icon.

It was necessary to overlook her talent, her intelligence, her ambition, because part of what men read into her and what indeed she presented was a child in woman's body—the breathy voice that so famously embodied that vulnerability, the inability to protect herself. She was presented as much as thing as woman in the gaze of the camera, whether film or still. There is a certain sadism aroused by all her incarnations, from Norma Jeane to "Marilyn." She recognized that victim radiance in herself. You cannot imagine her playing Joan Crawford's role in *Johnny Guitar*. She cannot attack. She cannot even defend. She can suffer, she can be protected, she can wish and yearn. But hidden in all that white breathiness is a woman who survived rape and abuse, being handed from powerful man to powerful man like a bottle of vodka, and who wanted and studied hard to be a good actress.

She seems at once to flaunt herself and to cringe within her shell. She creates in us a power as she seems powerless, the sense that she exists to be looked at, to be consumed by the public and the private gaze. If she is not looked at, not desired, not consumed by our gaze, she may disappear; and she did. We do not imagine her making speeches or walking a picket line or supporting candidates, although she had politics. We may define her by her absence or desire to be absent: her famous tardiness, her desire to escape the gaze that defined her, the many suicide attempts and the ambiguity about the final successful act—whether it was one more gesture that got out of hand, or a completed act.

One thing that may strike a woman upon viewing her old movies is that she was one of the last female stars who had a woman's natural body. She would be told now immediately to go on a strict diet and sent for liposuction, because we are no longer supposed to look womanly. Today's stars are carved and bony. She jiggled. She swayed. She was ripe and succulent. If she had bones, they were buried in flesh. She was flesh made luminous. Muscles, bones, sinews, they were there but unimportant in the message of flesh and skin, the softest moon glowing out of her ridiculous dresses. A woman could look at her and admire the sugar cake "Marilyn"—the artifact of bleach and the expert teasing of a hairdresser, the makeup, the foundation like an iron maiden, the dresses she was sewn into—and still feel that on a good day and with kind lighting "I could look like that." Because a woman could be sure that she could exude some of that appeal in her natural body. Few women can feel that confidence about the size-zero icons of today. It was opulence, not discipline and starvation that Marilyn Monroe embodied, but a tainted opulence for other women.

The women she played were totally unreal. Her vulnerability in her flesh was as compelling and audible as a baby crying, but she played either a gold digger—the woman who can only be bought—or the child/whore who asks nothing whatsoever, who is available like a tray of hors d'oeuvres at a cocktail party. In *The Seven Year Itch* she is the total male fantasy of available snatch, a gorgeous woman without any entanglements, no friends, no family, no demands, who wants only a married man since he won't fall in love with her. What living woman could ever identify with that character?

She was valued for her face and its beauty, certainly, but far more she was desired for her body. A woman whose body is desired while she herself—her real past, her ambitions, her fears, her ideas—is ignored, develops a deeply ambivalent relationship with that body. It does not quite seem to belong to her, but rather to those who value it beyond her, and all she seems to have to offer them is that same body. It is always a fraught relationship, because the body bloats, grows or shrinks, has its own mind, produces a period (in her case, incredibly painful) or doesn't (her confessed many abortions); gets pregnant or refuses to; demands food, demands sleep and then refuses to enter it; worst of all, threatens to grow older, and will. Furthermore, she remembers when she was far from cherished, when she was scorned, mocked, abused, unwanted. That is who, she suspects, she really is, under this dress of skin that others want to touch. This body is what they all want, but she suspects herself of being a fraud, because inside is just her. Maybe that self-hatred and that wearing of the body as total presentation was the reason she could not reach orgasm. She had to please; she did not deserve pleasure.

I remember a friend and I hearing ourselves on the radio in the late '60s, when we were putting on the Students for a Democratic Society radio show in New York, and discovering how like little girls we sounded. We worked very hard to get rid of those high voices and those helpless, mirthless girlish giggles, because we wanted to be taken seriously. So did she, but to abandon the façade of cotton candy would be to lose all that had made her successful and desirable.

Her career began with the famous nude calendar, although the most lasting images are at once dressed and undressed—the pose on the subway grating, for instance. She wears a flimsy looking halter dress that flies up, deserting her. She is the embodiment of titillation. Any man can dream of possessing her, because she seems so accessible and defenseless. For a man, that image on which can be projected any fantasy, any wish fulfillment, is the source of her immense and lasting appeal. She is a living doll—the perfect body that offers everything and asks nothing. She embodies the woman who never was because she isn't anything in herself. That image was something she put on to go out into the frightening and hostile world. She had learned early that she would be rewarded if she appeared compliant and childlike, not in the sense of the virgin to be deflowered, but in the sense of the woman who doesn't understand, doesn't know what to do, never learns a lesson; the warm and sensual Galatea who never gets up and leaves Pygmalion, but waits passively for the next owner. But behind that façade was a woman needy, scared, ambitious, leaking self-hatred and desperately wanting something real and solid and important. She wanted to be . . . respected. She never was.

Nice words for ugly acts

Downsizing: it sounds like losing weight.
Who in this body-crazy society doesn't
dream of getting skinny? But although
corporations are now people and surely
count more in elections that our lowly
bodies, that weight is individuals
whose families depend on those wages,
now about to lose their homes.

Outsource sounds so bland and tidy.
Nobody can hear the snap of breaking
lives, someone who had pride in his
or her job well done reduced to greeting
at Walmarts or flipping burgers or worse,
nothing at all but the TV all day with
depression moving in like an unwanted
dirty tenant who pays no rent.

These decisions are made invisibly.
Unlike the overseer who wields a whip,

unlike the pirate with his canons,
unlike even the mugger out of the dark—
faceless executives in their towers
mete out slow death, hunger, murder
of family, heart attack and stroke
with the stroke of a computer key.

WHY SPECULATE ON THE FUTURE?

TRYING TO FIGURE OUT what things will be like in a thousand years is a silly and futile endeavor, but it is also absorbing. If people did not enjoy imagining the future, there would be no science fiction and no speculative writing. We almost always guess wrong. My favorite short story of William Gibson is "The Gernsbach Continuum," in which a man finds himself in the future projected by 1930s designers—what he calls "raygun Gothic"—a future that never happened instead of our own: the world projected by the World's Fair as World War II was just beginning in Europe.

Imagine a monk in an abbey in England in AD 1000 trying to decide what the world would be like in the year 2000. Yes, there are still people, dogs, cats, horses, cows, and that's about it. The forests that covered much of England have vanished. Sherwood Forest has a few trees more than Manhattan—if you leave out Central Park. The monk's world was governed by the natural cycle of light and seasons and the cycle of the Catholic Church. He would not understand a single commercial or a book he would pick up—except perhaps some poetry. Poetry changes with every generation, but it does not improve or progress. It just changes its styles, trappings and some of its obsessions, but we can still enjoy

Sappho and Homer; they are today's news as much as when they were written—or recited.

The reason for speculation is more to consider options in the present than it is to predict the future with reliability. People have enough trouble predicting the stock market for the next six months or six weeks, or the likelihood of a marriage combination working out in two years. But that doesn't stop anyone from taking a flier in the market or getting married. From the moment we pick up the phone to talk to someone or walk out the door in the morning, we are taking chances—some with the odds in our favor and some really long shots. We attempt to predict the near future constantly and our future next year, next decade, twenty years hence in order to make plans involving work, houses, finances, retirement; but we know such planning is more hope than accuracy.

Truthfully, the most fruitful ways to approach the future for me are speculative fiction or utopian fiction. Isaac Asimov once said that all science fiction falls into three categories: What if, If only, and If this continues. I have written in all three categories. *Dance the Eagle to Sleep* is a kind of What if. *Woman on the Edge of Time* is mostly If only, with the brief venture into the dystopia of If this continues. *He, She and It* is If this continues. To me, fiction is my only legitimate access to future possibilities, because it admits that it is "made up" and is the fruit of imagination.

In the nineteenth and early twentieth centuries and again in the seventies of the twentieth century, a number of feminist utopias were created. I notice that in recent years, fewer of them are appearing. I believe that the urge to create them, while it comes from a sense of what we do not have in our lives, depends upon a certain ambient optimism or sense of movement and hope. When women are politically active in a way that seems to bring forward motion, then we have more energy and more desire to speculate about the kind of society we might particularly like to live in. When most of our political energy goes into defending gains we have made that are under attack, whether we are defending the existence of women's studies, access to safe medical abortions or affirmative action, there seems to exist among us less creative energy for imagining a fully realized alternative to what surrounds us.

The utopias that men have created over the centuries tend to be tremendously organized down to the street plans, tend to be hierarchical: cities of god where everything is minutely planned and perfectly utilized. The utopias women imagine tend to be looser, more fluid groupings where women can do things forbidden us, anarchical places of hard work and new means of giving birth, socializing children, finding companionship, love and sex, with different attitudes toward aging.

All feminist utopias spend a great deal of time worrying about child care—as women do in real life. I cannot think of a utopia created by a woman where a woman is solely responsible for her offspring. None of them contain that awful isolation many women report as occurring after birth when they find themselves left alone with a stranger, a new live baby who demands everything at the top of his or her lungs. One characteristic of societies imagined by feminists is how little isolated women are from one another. Instead of the suburban dream turned nightmare in which each house contained a woman alone and climbing the walls, or the yuppie apartment house where no one speaks but each has perfect privacy in her little electronic box, the societies women dream up tend to be long coffee klatches. Everybody is in everybody else's hair.

We live in a society in which many people report that their closest relationships are with their pets or with personages or characters they see on television. I understand the person/animal bond. My cats are friends. If I can't share my poems or my worries with them as I do with human friends, can't argue politics, neither are they too busy to give me their time and affection. But I can't imagine feeling intimacy with someone encountered on television. I write that, and a moment later I remember my mother's later years isolated in Florida where she knew no one, with a husband contemptuous of her. She was starved for conversation and interaction, so she would watch the evening news and argue with the anchors and reporters. Sometimes any simulacrum of communication and exchange has to satisfy us, because we can't get anything better.

Another characteristic of feminist utopias: freedom from fear of rape and domestic violence. All of them seek to eliminate domination of one person over another. People live in small groups, larger than nuclear families and less closed in, but small enough for everyone to know everyone else, as in extended families. Society is decentralized. Order is kept far more by persuasion than by force. Nurturing is a strong value. Communal responsibility for a child begins at birth.

These feminist visions tend to be ecologically conscious, assuming a partnership between the natural and the social world—excluding, of course, the older ones such as Charlotte Perkins Gilman's *Herland*. Often the societies women have imagined are quite pastoral. This is no accident, since what I view as one of the many functions of feminist art is to create that experience of the underlying ground of unity, among women, among all living creatures, among all of us who with our planet make up one being, Earth as she rolls along.

The societies portrayed in feminist visionary novels are usually communal, even quasi-tribal. Often a strong emotional connection to the natural world is stressed as a basis for an ecologically sound society. In James Tiptree's short story (James Tiptree was Alice Sheldon) "Houston, Houston Do You Read Me?" the spaceship of a feminist society contains not only chickens but an enormous kudzu vine, and the women who run the ship are excited about getting a goat soon.

One concern of *He, She and It* is what we are doing to the world we inherit and pass on, and what that will really mean to the daily lives of ordinary people. One of the strongest messages that we all receive through our pores, as well as through our ears and eyes from the media, is that ordinary necessary work is demeaning and those who do that work are fools and that ordinary people are made of inferior stuff and only the extraordinary, the celebrities, are made of different stuff. Fame is an attribute of the body and soul that ennobles through and through.

The only work that ennobles is unnecessary work, for example media work or financial manipulation. One of the most lucrative activities in our culture is taking over functioning companies that actually make something, playing with the stock and then moving them off to Guam or dismantling them altogether. This destruction is highly rewarded by our society. Feminist utopias are almost all concerned with the dignity of necessary work, as they tend to be concerned with integrating the aging into society and with socializing children as a mutual and glad responsibility.

Similarly, classlessness is pervasive in feminist visionary fiction, especially that written in this century. Many of the utopian novels women have written are deeply concerned with sharing the prestigious, the interesting, the rewarding opportunities, and also with sharing the maintenance, the housework, the daily invisible labor that underlies society.

Another characteristic of contemporary utopias is sexual permissiveness. The point of that permissiveness is not to break taboos but to separate sexuality from questions of ownership, reproduction and social structure. The feminist utopias that are not entirely lesbian often assume, as in Ursula Le Guin's *The Dispossessed*, some mix of monogamy, casual promiscuity, homosexuality and heterosexuality, with adolescent bisexuality as the norm. Many feminist utopias portray lesbian relationships matter-of-factly and without apology. For a number of them, lesbian relationships are the norm, since the societies described contain only women, such as Sally Miller Gearhart's *Wanderground*. *Herland* was probably the last asexual utopia created by a woman.

Some of these imagined societies emphasize sex as connection. These tend to be the ones that have an essentialist view of women as inherently nurturers. Others emphasize pleasure. They envision women's sexual energy loosed and free to redefine sexuality individually and collectively.

Some feminist utopias contain men and some do not. None of them contain men as we commonly think of men today, as the dominant, normative head of society. In none of them will you find a power structure that in any way resembles the Congressional committees that have lately been debating a woman's right to terminate an abortion when the fetus is not viable or when her life or health is threatened. As Joanna Russ suggests in her title *The Female Man*, women are the norm.

In general all utopian fiction seeks to create a society with an entirely different class structure (such as Plato's Republic), usually with the writer's social class having more power than is the case in the contemporary set-up—in Plato's case, in his Athens. But most feminist utopias seek to destroy class roles in the interest of equality.

Who wants equality? Those who do not have it.

Joanna Russ has written in "Recent Feminist Utopias":

> I believe that utopias are not embodiments of universal human values, but are reactive; that is, they supply in fiction what their authors believe society lacks in the here and now. The positive values stressed in the stories can reveal to us what, in the authors' eyes, is wrong with our society. Thus if the stories are familial, communal in feelings, we may safely guess that the authors see our society as isolating people from each other, especially (to judge from the number of all-female utopias in the group) women from women. If the utopias stress a feeling of harmony and connection with the natural world, the authors may be telling us that in reality they feel a lack of such connection.

In a similar vein, we might say that the classlessness of feminist utopias issues from the insecurities, the competitiveness and the poverty women experience. In the society we all know, our own, women congregate on the bottom. We hold the lowest-paying jobs. We are huddled with our children in homeless shelters and battered women's shelters. We constitute the bulk of the elderly poor. We speak of the feminization of poverty, but behind that Latinate word are millions of households of women struggling to get through another week, choosing between paying for heat and buying food, neglecting their own teeth and chewing aspirin, if they can buy aspirin, so that their children may have cereal, if not milk to put on it. Then there are growing numbers of women not held by any house but out there without shelter or safety of any sort.

The utopias' sexual permissiveness and joyfulness are poignant comments on the actual conditions of sexuality for women: unfriendly, coercive, simply absent, reactive rather than initiating, and I might add, regarded as a function of young women but not of older women and never of old women. A valued place and continuing integration for the aging is another common concern in feminist utopias. The women who write them know that they will likely live long enough to grow first middle-aged and then old, and that this society scorns and demeans older women. The more you know and the wiser you grow, the less valuable you are considered to be.

In a society in which women commonly experience streets as potential mine fields of violence about to explode; in which a city apartment has to be fortified like Fort Knox to protect not wealth but just one's own body and life; in which the first sexual experience for many children is the abuse by someone in their own home from whom they could reasonably expect protection and secure affection; in which any date can turn into an attack—no wonder women dream of a society in which sex is a chosen pleasure, chosen by a woman.

In our society, aging in women is seen as shameful. We are enjoined not to develop, not to mature, not to spread out, not to age. The images we buy unreflectively kill some of us and cripple many more. We are now in a time when people spend hours a day pursuing a perfect body, which is defined as someone who photographs well, since the camera adds fifteen pounds to anyone. We are as puritanical about food and weight as previous generations were about sex. Fat is supposed to be a sign of weakness, indulgence, sin. It takes an enormous amount of time to try always to look younger than you are and to try to carry less weight than your body comfortably wants to carry. It is supposed to be healthy. It is certainly a replacement for educating your mind, developing your interests, becoming closer to other people. If you spent the amount of time a week you might spend on the pursuit of a prepubescent body on learning a foreign language, on writing something meaningful to yourself and to others, on practicing piano, on changing the society—this country would be a far different place.

I wonder why the media is pushing thinness, called fitness. Of course it is partly a class issue: any affluent woman can afford a trainer, time in a gym, fitness equipment at home, someone to fill in for her while she exercises. The ordinary working class woman may have two jobs, kids to care for on her own, and no money to spend on a health club or a NordicTrack.

Being thin is not cumulative and you can never rest. The French you learned at twenty returns easily if you go to France. Retired athletes go as rapidly to flab as anyone else. So it is a permanent occupation; and truthfully, the waitress who has what is judged by this year's standards as a perfect body is still a waitress and likely to remain so. The myth is that the young and pretty and thin inherit the earth, but it ain't necessarily so. More likely it is the kid who sits at the computer instead of running around the block. Fat and pimples never kept anyone from writing a superb novel or mapping a chromosome or making a million.

We judge women who have, we say, let themselves go. Go where? I cannot remember a recent utopia that accepted the common idea in our culture that a woman's value is primarily as a decorative object, perfectly preserved. Most such novels are concerned with reintegrating the age segregation so typical of our recent society; with finding value in experience that our society finds only in the unused body.

Utopia is work that issues from pain: it is what we do not have that we crave. It is the labor of hunger, just as images of feasts, roast legs of lamb, mountains of pies are. A book came out a couple of years ago consisting of recipes that women remembered in concentration camps, while they were being systematically starved to death. Utopia is where we are not that we long to go.

It is by imagining what we truly desire that we begin to go there. That is the kind of thinking about the future that seems to me most fruitful, most rewarding. I want a future in which women are not punished for having women's bodies, are not punished for desire or the lack of it, are viewed as independent protagonists in their own adventures—spiritual, intellectual, romantic, sexual, and creative adventures. That's one reason I read and write speculative fiction.

MY LIFE, MY BODY

MOST OF YOU READING this have never lived in a world before *Roe v. Wade* made abortion legal if not affordable or procurable for many women. If I could take you into my own experiences when I was young, you'd be entering a world as strange and barbaric as historical novels like my own *City of Darkness, City of Light*, in which an apprentice is hung by the neck until dead for stealing a loaf of bread. Women lived with a fear hard for us to understand now, when the possibility of pregnancy meant that desire or even true love might kill. To become pregnant when you did not want to be was to enter a world of illegality and danger, of uncertainty and pain.

What you faced then was forced motherhood, signing your baby away, or abortions carried out without anesthetics. There was also a very real fear of bringing shame on your family, of losing your scholarship or job, of being forced to drop out of school and perhaps not be able to return, and of ruining your relationships, of arrest and imprisonment, of accidental sterility, of infection and pain, of death. Even after death, shame could continue. Dying of an abortion would be a newspaper scandal, unless concealed—if the family were able to persuade the doctor to fudge the cause of death (heart stopped). I had a friend who died of a botched abortion, but her death certificate claimed otherwise. In the years of the twentieth century when abortion was illegal, it is estimated that 40 percent of maternal deaths were from botched or self-inflicted abortions. You could die a great many ways, of bleeding to death, of septicemia or tetanus.

When I was eighteen, putting myself through the University of Michigan with a scholarship for tuition only, poor and home for the summer to work a minimum-wage job, I found myself pregnant. I was unable to locate a doctor or anyone willing to abort me. I cannot convey to you how simply terrifying it was then to go to a gynecologist or a clinic to try to find out if you were pregnant, and then to ask if there was anything, anything they were willing to do. What you would get was a lecture and lot of posturing if you were lucky; if not, you might face charges if you were reported to the university or any other authority. Determined to continue college, I did it myself, which almost cost me my life. Jill's abortion in *Braided Lives* is as close to what I went through as I could manage to put down. I had no medical attention. In the Detroit working-class neighborhood where I grew up, teenage pregnancy seems to me in retrospect as common as it is now, but I never knew anyone who had an abortion in a hospital, a doctor's office, or even from someone who posed as a doctor. Basically, it was do it yourself or stay pregnant.

Lore about how to abort yourself was rife through the dormitories. Most purported remedies were dangerous or useless, and some downright lethal. It was the same way with contraception then. It was not legal for an unmarried women to get contraception in most states, and trying to do so meant to face humiliation at the least and perhaps sexual harassment. I remember my experience being fitted for a surgical cap in

England when I was twenty-one. For one thing, the attendants were friendly and helpful and they were women. Second, they thought it normal and a good idea that an unmarried woman would not want to get pregnant. I was American, a foreigner, and yet they were sweet to me, and it was cheap, being that ogre of socialized medicine always called up with a shudder in the States.

Often nowadays a young woman says to me that if the right to choose is repealed, her doctor will of course take care of her. This naive certainty comes from a lack of understanding of what illegality entails. The few doctors who did abortions safely, cleanly, and on a regular basis were protected by the local police, local governments, organized crime, or some combination. Those of us who did abortion referrals and helped women get abortions in those dangerous times remember such doctors fondly, but their very existence was due to corruption. If a "respectable" doctor agreed to perform an abortion, often he would not take any responsibility for consequences. If the woman hemorrhaged or became infected, he would not respond. I remember years ago in Chicago helping a woman who had had an abortion and began to hemorrhage. When I called her doctor, he hung up on me, saying he had never had such a patient. I had to pack her with ice and hold her hand, while fearing all through the long night that she would die, in which case not only would she be dead but I would be an accessory to a crime and go to prison. The police would find me with the corpse in my apartment of a woman guilty of what was considered a serious crime. From the time of my own do-it-yourself abortion, I kept a file of abortionists I had heard of, with their prices, their protocols, their phone numbers and sometimes safe houses. It was something I began doing then and did until we made abortion legal finally.

Mentioning Chicago brings to mind another often forgotten trauma of that dreary time, one I remember best in the story of a friend of mine. Married for some years, she desperately wanted a child. Finally she succeeded in becoming pregnant. She was thin and frail but delighted. Unfortunately, halfway through her pregnancy, she began to miscarry. She was in pain and bleeding heavily. Under the law forbidding termination of pregnancy, she was guilty until proven innocent of having aborted herself. No painkillers, no assistance was given her in the hospital, but rather she was treated as a suspected criminal—at a time when she was feeling close to suicidal over losing her baby. She was left in the hospital corridor, bleeding and in horrible pain. Many doctors, nurses, aides, patients passed her, but none spoke to her. She was devastated psychologically, and that was essentially the end of her marriage.

How did *Roe v. Wade* come about? Did the Supreme Court wake up one morning and say, "This is all pretty absurd. Let's help women instead of punishing them for being female"? No, it was women who created the underground networks of referrals and women who marched and shouted and fielded obscene phone calls and were bussed to state capitols and to Washington to lobby and march again and again. It was women who made crude posters of other dead women and who lettered banners on sheets and who screamed ourselves hoarse in the streets of cities and towns. We had male allies like Bill Baird, but it was us in the streets and in the halls of state legislatures and constantly writing and protesting and politicking that changed the law.

It is important to remember, whether you personally approve or disapprove of abortion, that other people will live their lives as best they can. Married women will make that decision with regard to the needs of the children they already have, their husband's desires and character, their family's economic status and the other burdens on their time and energy, whether their family can endure the woman's taking time off work to care for another baby. The legality or illegality of abortion determines more about whether such a woman survives her choice than whether she makes it.

The rhetoric that says that a woman is selfish if she has an abortion is short-sighted. It is often more selfish to bring into the world a baby you cannot care for, cannot love, cannot cherish or nurture. It is usually the same senators and congressmen who oppose a woman's control over her body who also oppose family leave programs, daycare provision, health care for children whose mothers cannot get it or cannot afford it, the provision of legal aid and medical assistance to those who cannot pay for either. The fetus is precious, but once the child is born, it's dog-eat-dog. And we all know which dogs end up well fed.

We certainly have an abundance of children born to single mothers now, with abortions legal and generally not prohibitively expensive, although a woman may have to travel a hundred miles or more to find a hospital or clinic that is willing to perform one. Fortunately, with the decay of the shame attached to bastardy (and that word itself fading from the language except as a curse word with no more of its original content adhering to it than "damned" evokes theological connotations, as in "that damned cat") having a baby alone is a much sunnier possibility today. Of course, although society may not punish illegitimacy as once it did, the economic hardship and the lack of services a woman alone with a child experiences are trouble enough. Women alone with children lead the statistics we call the feminization of poverty. Yet single mothers are often single not because they weren't married but because that marriage ended, as half of them do, and frequently the husband and father is gone is all respects. When a woman chooses to have a child, she has to know that the odds are good that no matter how much she may love the father of that child, he may not be around to help raise it.

Whether abortion is legal or illegal, large numbers of women will resort to it, whether you are talking about women in a hunting-and-gathering society or women in high-rises. Abortion is a necessary activity for our species, until and unless we can absolutely control our fertility, because we are bonded to our young for such a long time before they can carry out an independent existence. When we give birth, we are committing our time and our financial resources for at least the next eighteen and perhaps the next twenty-four years or beyond. There are always going to be times when a woman can make such a commitment, and times when she cannot.

Sex leads to pregnancy less certainly than sugar leads to tooth decay, but we do not think of punishing teenagers for eating fast food by withholding dental work. We will not prevent women from terminating undesired pregnancies by making abortion illegal, dangerous, and not infrequently fatal. We will simply increase the amount of misery and danger in our society.

For me, the right of a woman to choose whether or not to have a baby grow in her body is a basic human right, not negotiable, not deniable. Who doesn't own their bodies? Slaves and women. There is nothing more personal than the inside of your body. Having a baby is a wonderful experience for many women, but not when it is forced on her.

It is not as if birth were a self-enclosed experience. It is a several-hundred-thousand-dollar baby you may be carrying. It is going to change your life permanently. Even if you give the baby up for adoption, your life and your self-image and self-esteem will be quite different than it would have been. There is someone out there alive and kicking who is going to appear at some time and ask you, Why? Whatever choice you make, likely you have interrupted your education, your career path, and you have lowered your standard of living—perhaps drastically. A single mother raising a child is everybody's business. Did she slap her child? Into court with her. Did she take a job? Neglect. Did she fail to take a job? Welfare queen!

When I watch and listen to the Congress of the United States at once try to cut back abortion rights with the aim of eventually repealing them, at the same time that they cut off funds for contraception and refuse funds for day care and throw young and old women off welfare, I wonder if the problem isn't that the senators and congressmen feel that there are not enough sixteen-year-old prostitutes on the streets of Washington, DC. I can only conclude that that is the intent of their legislation. If you take a sixteen-year-old with a baby to support, do you really think she can do that with a job at McDonald's? And if she leaves her baby alone, you can get her for neglect. What a marvelous set of brutal punishments for being young and poor.

I recommend you read our congressmen talking about women who have abortions. Obviously they are a danger to the republic far greater than drug cartels or militiamen with rifles and bombs. The fear of a sexually active woman is extremely powerful. When I was in college, one of my good friends had a sister who was confined to a mental institution. Was she schizophrenic? No, she was sexually active at sixteen, and that was reason enough to put her away, treat her with electroshock and heavy drugging. It was a crime to be sexually active then, and we still have a portion of the population that talks about a sexually active woman as if she is on a par with child rapists and serial killers.

Abortions have not always been illegal. The Catholic Church did not even assume a position against them until the last couple of hundred years. Women's culture has often contained lore on how to prevent pregnancy and how to abort an unwanted fetus. Almost all cultures labeled primitive had technology that accomplished this quite efficiently. Having more than two children was so unusual among the Shawnee people of Ohio, for instance, that the great chief Tecumseh's mother was called what translates as Turtle Who Lays Her Eggs in the Sand—for it was felt among her tribe that she could not possibly care for her six children properly. Since she had had so many children, obviously she was like a turtle who simply deposited her offspring as eggs and happily departed. I was raised with the *stetl* morality of women that it was a woman's business to determine whether the family—and the welfare of the other children—could afford another child. No paternal consent was involved, because it was assumed to be not his concern or business, even in patriarchal families.

But choosing to have a baby or to terminate a fetus is only a right as long as there are doctors and technicians willing to perform abortions, and access to places where women may safely be examined, tested, prescribed contraceptives, and undergo whatever procedures are agreed upon by doctor and patient. The legal rights do not matter if you cannot get to a clinic. Ninety percent of women in the United States live a considerable distance from a clinic or hospital where abortions are performed. For them to get an abortion requires making some incredible excuse if they are underage, perhaps finding a ride if there is no available public transportation—a common occurrence in our culture, which expects every citizen to have an least one functional car. It may require cutting school. It may require missing one or more days of work. It may require all kinds of lying and excuses. I imagine it is a rare student who hands the counselor a note from her mother saying Mary could not come to school yesterday as she was off in Memphis having an abortion.

Even if you get yourself to a clinic, here are you, nervous, full of anxiety. You don't know if it will hurt. You've heard horror stories of regret, recrimination, and complications. Frankly, you're scared. Maybe you have a friend with you, maybe an understanding family member. Maybe your boyfriend or husband has accompanied you. More likely, you are alone. Determined but apprehensive. But there you are approaching the clinic, and what do you see? A crowd of rabid men and women with posters of six- and seven-month fetuses on long poles screaming at you, BABY KILLER! Large, hostile men try to block your path, threaten you, jostle you, perhaps even throw you to the ground.

But once you make your way in, you have run the gauntlet and you are safe. You are greeted gently by a receptionist and everything is calm. But what about the people who work there? What about the doctor who makes far less money than he would in a lucrative practice. My former gynecologist is on every kill list these haters put out. They print the names on the internet. They send them around to like-minded groups. They plant bombs. And they get guns and they shoot to kill. He had to close his private practice because he felt he could not protect his patients.

You should be aware that many medical schools have stopped teaching abortion procedures; that many hospitals are afraid to perform them, for fear of harassment. That many doctors refuse, not because they have any objections, but because they don't want to put themselves or their families in danger. That the Catholic Church is buying up hospitals that then refuse to deal with contraceptives or abortions. In some states, pharmacists have taken it upon themselves to refuse to fulfill prescriptions for the morning-after pill, because they have decided they personally do not approve of it.

I have many issues that press upon me, but regardless of record, I simply cannot vote for an antichoice candidate. I feel I would be voting for the destruction of the lives of women I have never met, for the abuse of children born unwanted, for families' economic ruin. I would be voting for pain and suffering I too often witnessed when terminating a pregnancy was illegal. I cannot do that. No matter what the economic or social or environmental issues, this is my bottom line on candidates. It is simply to me a matter of life and death.

Behind the war on women

Who does not control her own body?
A slave. Aging white men addicted
to power cannot stand girls and women
choosing for themselves. They dream

of bringing back those patriarchal days
when women in pearls like tiny teeth
rustling in taffeta brought platters
of Betty Crocker cakes, salads

of raisins, carrots and celery
in orange Jello to men who barely
needed to acknowledge their labor
because God willed it so. They want

the others crushed back into their
places, smiles glued on, costumes
intact, ready to serve as the punch-
lines of jokes shared over cigars.

Those were the days! And nights
of subservience only available now
if they pay for it. Their anger swells
until solidified into punitive laws

that will strip women of choice,
of their uppity freedoms, of life itself
to bring back those glorious father
knows best chastity belt years.

NEVER CATCH A BREAK

IN THE TWENTIETH CENTURY, as the political ferment surrounding the Great Depression died down in the patriotic surge surrounding World War II, a heresy emerged in critical thinking about writing (and painting, for that matter). It was widely legislated by critics and academics that writing that incorporated any push toward social change—writings, in other words, of the Left—was not to be considered serious work. Any such writings were mere polemics—as if all stories do not contain notions of what is good and what is bad for people; who are the heroes and who are the villains; who deserves to win and who to lose, and what are winning and losing, anyhow? Who is okay to make fun of and who should be revered? What is it okay to do in bed with whom and how? All stories contain such attitudes built into the writing, even if not overtly presented. When the values assumed in the writing are those of the established order, such works are not considered political. It is only when the values are counter to those with power that the work is dismissed as polemical.

Critics and reviewers still tend to review fiction that corresponds in its values to those they are used to hearing over dinner or reading in the Bible called *The New York Times* and discuss it

solely in terms of the quality of execution. Fiction that embodies different ideas and politics is therefore tainted and generally
denounced or dismissed. Reviewers only seem to notice opinions
that differ from their own; those they agree with are not opinions
but just the way things are, part of the quiet background.

But for thousands of years, most writers assumed that politics was part of life and had its place in literature. Blake, Shelley,
Victor Hugo, Zola, Alexander Pope, Milton, Shakespeare, Yeats,
Wordsworth, Byron, Tolstoy—whether of the Right or the Left,
all wrote with a consciousness of politics, because they were human beings, because they were members of society. Writers don't
exist in a vacuum. We are creatures of our time and place, the
class we were born into and/or identify with, the economic and
social pressures that limit or expand the opportunities and the
calamities we experience, what happens around us to our family
and friends and partners as well as ourselves. We are each more or
less aware of the forces that coerce us, that lie to us, that make us
ashamed, that determine what we are trying to get for ourselves
or others.

It takes determination and courage to write what your train-
ing, education and the attitudes of those with power over you
have insisted is without merit. It takes determination and courage
and attention to craft to figure out how to do well what you have
been told is not worth doing. All of us across the spectrum of the
Left struggle with these issues and problems. Some people with
strong politics attempt to keep them out of their writing and
pride themselves on doing so. But others of us do not buy into
the notion that writing that aims to change society is less valuable
than writing that upholds its values and customs.

In my own approach to fiction I am always balancing between my belief that story is primary and that the most basic

most primitive impulse in narrative (what then? when then? and then what?) is also the most sacred, and that narrative at base is about finding patterns in experience, both the recurring and the singular; and on the other hand, an equally passionate absorption in character and a belief that fiction is simply the expression of character in action in choice through time. I survive happily as a fiction writer with both of these contradictory theories and impulses and passions always active in me, and find my best ideas in this tension. I like and read work from both tendencies. I consider both approaches undervalued at present by a preference for certain styles and types of subject matter, rather a narrow range but able to be produced by the yard by any bright writing student with a yen for grants and approval.

The problem I have with the passive rather bland characters frequently found in contemporary fiction, the mental anorexics, is that I don't think passive characters are more realistic or more "American" than characters who take an active role in their own lives. On the other hand, I recognize that we are being trained from infancy into a people who expect to have images fed into us, with the attention span of a puppy and the intellectual curiosity of a stale doughnut. However, I have experienced the extraordinary rich and deep capacity of ordinary people many times in my life. It is that ability to open and grow that often exercises my imagination as a writer. I am interested in fiction involving characters who seize or are seized by the currents and necessities and opportunities of their particular time and place. I always see characters in history. I find that the lives of ordinary working people generate sufficient struggle, passion, hope, conflict, terror to sustain infinite fictional exploration.

I have written realistically and surrealistically and speculatively, and none of these modes command my loyalty and none seem to be any more faithful to the reality of living than any other mode. I am loyal to the story, and I find as much meaning in weird tales of dragons and androids as I do in tales of advertising men and dope dealers. To me the self is vast, amorphous, part animal, part collective, overlapping with others underground, tapping hidden rivers that flow through us.

Work by women is constantly undervalued and frequently ignored. Ever so often a white male writer will produce an essay that laments the absence of true political novels—ignoring the work that many women have published and are still writing; ignoring also the work of most nonwhite writers except for the one or two who are singled out and rewarded. Often even then the work that is prized is of a type that is not threatening, that cannot cause the literary establishment unease.

Ask yourself why *Moby Dick* is the great American novel, as I believe it to be. Ask why Mark Twain didn't send two white boys down the Mississippi. Ask why Dos Passos's novels are no longer considered important. Ask why often only science fiction takes on the most important issues and divides of our time: climate change, class structure, sex roles, oppression of those we regard as unlike us, genocide, our treatment of nonhuman animals, our culture of war.

Fiction is not something most people read any longer, and we wonder why.

PORT HURON CONFERENCE STATEMENT

THERE'S A GENERAL ASSUMPTION on the part of American critics and academics that anyone who writes fiction or poetry that is politically conscious must be kind of dense—that by its nature that work is cruder than work that simply embodies currently held notions; that leftist or feminist work is more naive, simpler, less profound than right-wing work. What is considered deep is writing that deals with man's fate (always man's) in psychospiritual terms, with our heart of darkness, somehow always darker when somebody is thinking that maybe things could be changed. Deep work deals with angst-filled alienation. Literature is perceived, as Hans Haacke said about art, "as a mythical entity above mundane interests and ideological conflict."

I've never been able to understand the assumption that being ignorant of science is good for poets, or that being ignorant of economics and social organization is good for novelists. I've always imagined that the more curious you are about the world around you, the more you'll have to bring to your characters and to the worlds that you spin around them. I've speculated that one reason too many American novelists haven't developed but, rather, have atrophied, producing their best work out of the concerns of late adolescence and early adulthood, is that since they do not care to grapple with or even to identify powerful forces in our society, they can't understand more than a few stories.

Writing that is politically conscious involves freeing the imagination, which is one reason why magic realism was so energizing to Latin American fiction. If we view the world as static, if we think ahistorically, we lack perspective on the lives we are creating. The more variables we can link and switch in the mind, the more we can examine the unconscious premises of our fiction and our poetry. We must be able to feel ourselves active in time and history. We choose from the infinitely complex past certain stories, certain epochs, certain struggles and battles, certain heroines and heroes that lead to us. We draw strength from them as we create our genealogy, both literarily and personally. Deciding who we are is intimately associated with who we believe our ancestors, our progenitors, our precursors are. That's one of the reasons I've written historical novels about the French revolution when modern feminism began, and about the tumultuous periods right after the American Civil War and throughout World War II. And because I want to explore possible futures and extrapolate from trends and activities pushing on us or originating from progressive movements, I write science fiction. And because I want to explore the lives of people in the here and now, I write contemporary novels.

In the arts, particularly, we need our own sense of lineage and our own tradition to work in or to rebel against. Often we must work in a contrapuntal way to a given genre or tradition, taking it apart, slicing it against the grain, making explicit its assumptions. Think of Margaret Atwood's use of the Gothic novel tradition.

A sense of false belonging destroys our ability to think and to feel. A seamless identification with a culture that excludes us as fully human or that impoverishes our options limits us. This is especially true in America, where official history is Disney World. Most of us are the grandchildren or children of immigrants, whether they came willingly or not, with parents who refused to speak whatever language was theirs as a birthright or were forbidden to use it, and who considered all the history and wisdom and stories of their families as so much peasant trash to be dumped and forgotten. Some of us had our lineage and even our names stolen from us. Often we have lost not only the names of the villages where our ancestors lived but any knowledge of what they did for a living, what they believed, why they left and came here or were forcibly brought. We have lost the history of labor and religious struggles they may have bled for. This ignorance makes us shallower than we may want to be. That's why when someone like Thai Jones writes about the anarchists in New York City in the decade before World War I, it's important. We can learn as much from the mistakes others made as we can from their successes.

Reviewers don't perceive books as having a political dimension when the ideas expressed in those works are congruent with the reviewers' own attitudes or with those they're used to hearing discussed over supper or at parties. When reviewers read fiction or poetry whose attitudes offend them or clash with their own ideas, they perceive those works as political and polemical, and they attack them. This can also happen on the Left, when a particular work doesn't satisfy the ideology of the reviewer. It's always far easier to fight someone with whom you share 85 percent of your politics than someone who shares 50 percent or less. Organizing inside a movement is easier too than actually organizing the uncommitted; but is, of course, far less useful.

Furthermore, the importance of imagination arises from the need to strive for something better than more of the same: please, not bigger Big Macs, more powerful SUVs, wider and wider flat screen TVs, huger McMansions. Speculative fiction enables the reader to enter worlds in which important variables have changed or in which current trends are extrapolated and we can see the full danger and damage. Much science fiction wastes this opportunity by creating princes and princesses and worlds in which our prejudices are written large. But at its best, science fiction can shake our assumptions or spell them out for us so that we can more easily, more fully examine them.

In a stratified society all literature is engaged politically and morally, whether it's so perceived by the author or not. It will be so perceived by the readers it validates and by the readers it affronts. This doesn't mean that I think a novel or a poem can be judged purely by utilitarian criteria. Literature is only partly rational. It acts on all the levels of our brain and influences us through sounds and silences, through identification and imagery, through rhythms and chemistry. Telling stories is an ancient human activity because it's partly how we make sense of the world, how we find patterns in our lives and the lives of those who came before us and we hope will come after us. It's how we construct a meaningful world. Stories make patterns where otherwise there would be chaos.

But as writers and readers, the literature we read makes us more or less sensitive to each other. Poems and novels tell us how we may expect to experience love and hatred, violence and peace, birth and death. They deeply influence what we expect to find as our love object, and what we expect to enjoy on the job or in bed, and what we think is okay for others to enjoy. They help us decide what war is like—a boring hell destroying other people's countries and lives as well as our own soldiers' lives; or a necessary masculine maturation experience in a peer group. They cause us to expect that rape is a shattering experience of violence, like being struck by a hit-and-run truck, or a titillating escapade that all women secretly desire. They influence our daydreams and our fantasies and therefore what we believe other people offer us or are withholding from us.

Art doesn't progress the way physics progresses. In art we don't build better bombs. We don't know more about poetry than Sappho did, or tell a better story than Homer did. If a poem or story works, it's new. It's new always. It's made again. Like love. Like anger. We have to be true to our own experiences and those we can empathize with, whether they are experiences the society expects from us or whether they may end up labeled bizarre or deviant. One generation's outcasts may become another generation's heroes and heroines.

For me, writing fiction issues from the impulse to tell the stories of people who deserve to have their lives examined and their stories told to people who deserve to read good stories. I'm responsible to many people with buried lives, people who have been rendered as invisible in history as they are powerless in the society. For me the impulse to write poems comes from the desire to give permanent voice to something in the experience of a life. To speak memorably in a way that moves and enlightens and fixes the ephemeral in something at least quasi-permanent. To find ourselves spoken for in poetry gives dignity to our pain, our anger, our lust, our losses. We can hear what we hope for, and what we most fear, in the small release of cadenced utterances. We have few rituals that function as well for us in the ordinary chaos of our lives as art can. The pattern, imposed perhaps but nonetheless satisfying, emerges from the utterance, from the story.

I think of poetry as utterance that heals the psyche because of the way it uses verbal signs and images, sound and rhythm, memory and dream images, blending all the different kinds of knowing, the analytical and the synthetic, the rational and the prerational and the gestalt grasping of the new or ancient configurations. For the moment of experiencing a poem, we may be healed to our diverse selves, connecting thinking, feeling, seeing, remembering, dreaming.

Fiction is as old a habit of our species as poetry. It goes back to telling a tale, the first perceptions of pattern, and fiction is still about pattern in human life. At core, it answers the question, what then? And then and then and then. I have tried to figure out, coming into postmodern poetry and fiction, exactly why people have carried out these activities, what they are supposed to do, why I engage in them and why others should pay attention to what I produce. Fiction is about time. First this, then that. Or this, then before it was that. Therefore this. From the perception of the seasons, of winter, spring, summer, fall, of the seasons of our lives, of the things that return and the things that do not return, of the drama of the search and finding of the fruit, the seed, the root that sustains life, the looking and the hunting and the kill, the arc of the sex act, the climax of giving birth: these are the sources of the fictional intelligence. If you make such a choice (being kind to an old woman on the road, marrying Bluebeard against all advice, apprenticing yourself to a witch), what follows?

It isn't a matter of a concrete agenda. In his analysis of the Occupy movement, Steven Duncombe talks about what the image of countless signs and myriad demands says about what a good, pluralistic, truly democratic society would look like. Freeing the imagination is one of the functions of literature, and one reason why academia and the givers of prizes reward poetry that speaks to and moves no one but people writing theses or adding to their publishing resumes. Literature can be dangerous to the status quo, no matter in how minor a way. It is part of the conspiracy to remove meaning from art. When I was younger, we were always getting quoted at us the phrase by Archibald MacLeish: A poem should not mean, but be. Like a vase, I guess. Something to admire and walk on by. It can't impact you in any way. I'm not referencing the way teachers approach poetry as if a poem were some weird way of delivering a message, or a puzzle or that must be ferreted out and decoded, but because what poems mean emotionally, culturally and directly is part of what they are doing—only a part, but an important part.

Shelley called poets the unacknowledged legislators of the world, but that was nonsense. In the arts, we do not generally have much influence on public policy. Polemics can fire up the already persuaded, posters can make people aware of your opinion, much like bumper stickers. But what we do is change consciousness a tiny bit at a time. Through fiction, we enable people to walk in someone else's shoes, boots, moccasins for a few hours, which may persuade us that the Others as we define them are human too. Poetry readings can give us a sense, no matter how momentary, of community, as liturgy does. To claim that art has a use is not the same as claiming that art can be evaluated only in terms of that use. The meeting of the rational and the irrational, the healing that art can perform in the individual and the collective psyche, are not wholly explicable. Art, even in words, is not capable of being discussed entirely with words. Poetry can at once be called useful, and mysterious. What heals one person may not heal another.

As writers we are always asking in public through our work whether our experiences and those of other people with whom we empathize and from whom we create, are experiences common to at least part of the population; or whether the experiences we are working with are crazy, singular, bizarre. There are inner censors that make shallow or imitative or tentative or coy the work of a writer, often through fear.

Voices speak in our heads that tell us that we are brazen to admit certain things, that we should be ashamed. We may fear to offend those with power over us or hurt those whom we wish to love us or those whom we wish to please. We may fear what those whose politics or religion we share and whose good opinion we rely on may say about work which deals with a contradiction in our mutual politics or religious values, and the contradictions between ideology or belief and action. Yet such contradictions are rich to writers. Writing that is politically conscious involves freeing the imagination, for if we view the world as static, if we think ahistorically, we lack perspective.

Societies differ in how they regard the artist, how integrated into the ordinary work of the community she is regarded or encouraged to regard herself as being. We may be artists, but we are also citizens with the same responsibility as every other citizen.

Poems are often produced in a person or a group's process of coming to consciousness of their identity and their oppression. Think of the outpouring of African-American poetry when Black Power and Black Pride were emerging. Think of the poetry that burst from the second wave of women's liberation. Good poetry can come out of prison.

But being political is only part of our personhood, along with our physical bodies and health or frailty, our group identifications, our family history and identity, our ethnicity, our race, our religion or spirituality, the friends and lovers we choose, the animals we live with and care for, our sense of our environment, the teams we care about, the food we choose or cannot choose to eat, the music we listen to. Art relates to many of the rich and conscious or unconscious aspects of our lives and the Left should respect it more than it commonly does. Literature, if we bother to read and support it, has power and it can help us survive and win.

Who has little, let them have less

The hatred of the poor, is it guilt
gone rancid? That the rich have
so much and still conspire to steal
a baby's medicine, a woman's
life, a man's heart and kidney.

When those Congressmen talk
of people who are counting
their last change for gas or eggs
choosing between cold and hunger
they snarl. How dare we exist?

If they could push a button,
if they could war on the poor
here at home as they do abroad
directly with bombs instead of
legislation, think they'd hesitate?

The righteous anger fermenting
in them boils over in cuts to what-

ever keeps people alive. They punish
those who have little with less:
a vast legal bus to run us over.

NOVELS

Sex Wars
The Third Child
Three Women
Storm Tide (with Ira Wood)
City of Darkness, City of Light
The Longings of Women
He, She and It
Summer People
Gone to Soldiers
Fly Away Home
Braided Lives (republished 2013)
Vida (republished 2011)
The High Cost of Living
Woman on the Edge of Time
Small Changes
Dance the Eagle to Sleep (republished 2011)
Going Down Fast

OTHER WORKS

The Cost of Lunch, Etc. (A collection of short stories)
Pesach for the Rest of Us
Sleeping with Cats: A Memoir
So You Want to Write: How to Master the Craft of Writing Fiction and Personal Narrative (with Ira Wood), 1st & 2nd editions
Parti-Colored Blocks for a Quilt: Essays
The Last White Class: A Play (with Ira Wood)
Early Ripening: American Women's Poetry Now: An Anthology

BIBLIOGRAPHY

POETRY

Made in Detroit
The Hunger Moon: New & Selected Poems
The Crooked Inheritance
Colors Passing Through Us
The Art of Blessing the Day
Early Grrrl
What Are Big Girls Made Of?
Mars and Her Children
Available Light
My Mother's Body
Stone, Paper, Knife
Circles on the Water (Selected Poems)
The Moon Is Always Female
The Twelve-Spoked Wheel Flashing
Living in the Open
To Be of Use
4-Telling (with Bob Hershon, Emmett Jarrett, and Dick Lourie)
Hard Loving
Breaking Camp

ABOUT THE AUTHOR

MARGE PIERCY IS THE author of seventeen novels including the *New York Times* bestseller *Gone to Soldiers*; the national bestsellers *Braided Lives* and *The Longings of Women* and the classic *Woman on the Edge of Time*; nineteen volumes of poetry; a collection of short stories, *The Cost of Lunch, Etc.*; and a critically acclaimed memoir, *Sleeping with Cats*.

Born in center-city Detroit, educated at the University of Michigan and Northwestern University, and the recipient of four honorary doctorates, she has been a key player in many of the major progressive political battles of our time, including the anti–Vietnam War and the women's movement, and more recently an active participant in the resistance to the wars in Iraq and Afghanistan.

Praised as one of the few American writers who are accomplished poets as well as novelists—Piercy is one of the country's bestselling poets—she is also the master of many genres: historical novels, science fiction, novels of social comment and contemporary entertainments. She has taught, lectured, and performed her work at over four hundred fifty universities, festivals, and fundraisers around the world.

Available from PM Press

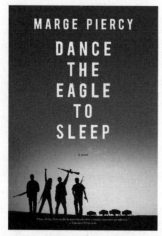

Braided Lives
978-1-60486-442-7
$20.00

The Cost of Lunch, Etc.
978-1-62963-125-7
$15.95

Dance the Eagle to Sleep
978-1-60486-456-4
$17.95

Vida
978-1-60486-487-8
$20.00

FRIENDS OF

These are indisputably momentous times—the financial system is melting down globally and the Empire is stumbling. Now more than ever there is a vital need for radical ideas.

In the eight years since its founding—and on a mere shoestring—PM Press has risen to the formidable challenge of publishing and distributing knowledge and entertainment for the struggles ahead. With hundreds of releases to date, we have published an impressive and stimulating array of literature, art, music, politics, and culture. Using every available medium, we've succeeded in connecting those hungry for ideas and information to those putting them into practice.

Friends of PM allows you to directly help impact, amplify, and revitalize the discourse and actions of radical writers, filmmakers, and artists. It provides us with a stable foundation from which we can build upon our early successes and provides a much-needed subsidy for the materials that can't necessarily pay their own way. You can help make that happen—and receive every new title automatically delivered to your door once a month—by joining as a Friend of PM Press. And, we'll throw in a free T-shirt when you sign up.

Here are your options:

- $30 a month: Get all books and pamphlets plus 50% discount on all webstore purchases
- $40 a month: Get all PM Press releases (including CDs and DVDs) plus 50% discount on all webstore purchases
- $100 a month: Superstar—Everything plus PM merchandise, free downloads, and 50% discount on all webstore purchases

For those who can't afford $30 or more a month, we're introducing Sustainer Rates at $15, $10, and $5. Sustainers get a free PM Press T-shirt and a 50% discount on all purchases from our website.

Your Visa or Mastercard will be billed once a month, until you tell us to stop. Or until our efforts succeed in bringing the revolution around. Or the financial meltdown of Capital makes plastic redundant. Whichever comes first.

PM Press was founded at the end of 2007 by a small collection of folks with decades of publishing, media, and organizing experience. PM Press co-conspirators have published and distributed hundreds of books, pamphlets, CDs, and DVDs. Members of PM have founded enduring book fairs, spearheaded victorious tenant organizing campaigns, and worked closely with bookstores, academic conferences, and even rock bands to deliver political and challenging ideas to all walks of life. We're old enough to know what we're doing and young enough to know what's at stake.

We seek to create radical and stimulating fiction and non-fiction books, pamphlets, t-shirts, visual and audio materials to entertain, educate, and inspire you. We aim to distribute these through every available channel with every available technology—whether that means you are seeing anarchist classics at our bookfair stalls; reading our latest vegan cookbook at the café; downloading geeky fiction e-books; or digging new music and timely videos from our website.

PM Press is always on the lookout for talented and skilled volunteers, artists, activists, and writers to work with. If you have a great idea for a project or can contribute in some way, please get in touch.

PM Press
PO Box 23912
Oakland CA 94623
510-658-3906
www.pmpress.org